Letters
to
Half Moon
Street

Letters to Half Moon Street

A Romance

By
Sarah Wallace

Book One in Meddle & Mend

Print ISBN: 978-1-7374327-0-8

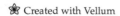 Created with Vellum

For those who need the reminder: you are enough.
This book is for you.

FROM GERALDINE HARTFORD
   Shulfield Hall, Tutting-on-Cress
TO GAVIN HARTFORD
   8 Half Moon Street, London

28 August 1815

DEAR GAVIN,

Mama has written to me about her scheme to send you to London. I thought having a letter waiting for you when you arrive might be a pleasant surprise. You will likely be a grump about the whole thing for you do not enjoy having your life upset, but surely you will not want to be at home when John and Veronica take over the house. You and John have never gotten along in the best of circumstances. Living together while his wife goes through her confinement will only exacerbate things. Goodness knows what sort of chaos will ensue when her baby is actually born. Mama is quite right to send you away. You know I do not say that lightly.

Before you ask, no, I will not come and help you settle in London. I am having a capital time with our cousins and have no interest in leaving.

I believe living alone in town will do you some good. You want a little independence, my dear brother. Please do not spend all of your time in the library.

And do try to enjoy yourself.

Affectionately,

Gerry

FROM GAVIN HARTFORD
 8 Half Moon Street, London
TO GERALDINE HARTFORD
 Shulfield Hall, Tutting-on-Cress

1 September 1815

GERRY,

London is already a right bore. If you were a kind sister, like you ought to be, you would not make me suffer alone. Terribly unsporting of you.

Mother was in a fine state before I left. She had the servants going through all the usual household spells, making sure every part of the house was spotless. I don't see why she bothers. Veronica is happiest when she feels superior, so a less than perfect house will make her more eager than ever to be mistress of it someday.

When Mother first suggested this scheme, I thought she was sending me to London only to get me out of the house temporarily. But it seems she intends for me to stay until after the baby is born. She even said I might as well stay for six months or more. She has insisted I will be in the way. It is absurd for her to be in such a state. Veronica is unlikely to actually take Mother's advice on anything, and will only frustrate everybody.

Oh, and Father sat me down and went over all of the business he wants me to take care of while I am in London. I suppose I should be grateful he did not foist these responsibilities upon me sooner. And I daresay I'm glad I'm not the firstborn. Having that much responsibility would be even worse, even with the benefit of inheritance. At any rate, Father said the real reason I am staying here is to see to it that the townhouse is prepared for the Season, and he gave me a list of things he wants taken care of. He also said if I do well enough at all of this, I might be able to continue with it as an actual career—acting as steward on John's behalf. I shudder to imagine it. I really must find an occupation for myself, and soon. I did notice Father did not alter the timeline Mother put forth. So I suspect this list of responsibilities is merely to keep me busy. What a great bother it all is.

Our townhouse in London was outrageously warm when I arrived. I'm glad I wasn't sent here at the height of the summer. As it was, I had to dash around the house to help the servants open the windows. Then I had to set up at least a dozen cooling spells. Cook already needs more mint for the purpose. I still have that tendency to overload my spells with too much magical power, so the cooling spells ought to have made the place frigid. And yet, it is still too warm. It would be far better if you were here to help me.

I confess I am thoroughly intimidated by the city. Father gave me directions to the club we're members of. I had initially planned to walk there. I'm accustomed to walking or riding everywhere back at home, but I am far too nervous about getting lost. I took a hackney the first time I went to Nesbit's Club, and I was immediately confused by all the turns and the traffic. I am sure you will scold me, but I cannot countenance going anywhere other than the club at this juncture.

Did you go to Nesbit's when you were in town? I own I did not know what to expect. I liked the quiet atmosphere, but I was alarmed by the number of people inside. I went straight to the dining room and found a little table in the corner. I sat next to a lovely stained glass window, which was pleasant, and no one approached me, which was a relief. It was unsettling, though, to sit in a dining room amongst strangers and to be completely alone.

Now I am alone in London and it may be months before I can leave. Until the Season begins in earnest, there is precious little to do. Not that I would relish being here when the Season is at its peak, for you know I do not enjoy suffering through so much society. Even with Father's list of responsibilities, I am not exactly busy. I daresay I'm grateful for that, but I feel sure I shall forget something. Practically all I have to occupy my time is to dine at Nesbit's Club, which is hardly diverting. At home, I could hide in books all day, but the library in our London house is nothing to the library at home. It would serve our parents right if I gambled away my funds out of sheer boredom.

Give my regards to our cousins.

Affectionately,

Gavin

FROM GERALDINE HARTFORD
Shulfield Hall, Tutting-on-Cress
TO GAVIN HARTFORD
8 Half Moon Street, London

4 September 1815

DEAR GAVIN,

You know Mama. Once she has a scheme in her head she must have her way.

Do you remember when our cousin said Tutting-on-Cress was simply filled with eligible bachelors? Now that I am here, I am convinced Rose was fibbing. There are precious few single men around. Besides, I'm fairly sure Rose fancies another woman in the village. So I have no idea why she was even considering gentlemen suitors. From what Aunt Lily has said, there was some sort of to-do in the spring—something about a dashing bachelor. Rose has been tight-lipped on the details, but I suppose it's possible for her to be of the feminine persuasion and still have her head turned by a particularly handsome man. If I learn more, I shall tell you.

In any case, attempting to win a husband is an exhausting

experience. So I'm not opposed to simply enjoying my time here, rather than continuing the search. I have not admitted any of this to Mama yet. I think she will be disappointed about the lack of prospective suitors, but I doubt she will mind me staying here indefinitely. She trusts me to behave well around John even less than she trusts you. You will simply grumble and lock yourself up in the library. But suffering under John's company, I might actually put a curse on him, brother or no.

You cannot convince me there is nothing for you to do. Is there no one you can talk to at our club? You do know Nesbit's caters to the intellectual set, don't you? I'm sure you could find someone there who shares an interest in poetry or magic or something. Of course, you would have to actually talk to them to discover this. I certainly hope you do not intend to spend your entire time in London without talking to anybody.

I agree with you on the subject of the library in the townhouse. Try Hatchard's Bookshop. They kept me quite afloat while I was in London.

I don't believe you would be such a pinhead as to gamble away your money. But I think it might do you some good to be reckless, so I will not talk you out of it. I warn you, however, that I shall not lend you my money. The shops in Tutting-on-Cress are excellent, despite it being a small town, and there are plenty of things I wish to buy.

Affectionately,
Gerry

FROM GAVIN HARTFORD
   8 Half Moon Street, London
TO GERALDINE HARTFORD
   Shulfield Hall, Tutting-on-Cress

7 September 1815

GERRY,

You may not believe it, but I have already completed Father's list. Well, some of the items must be repeated throughout my stay, but I have managed to take care of everything else. I suppose Father may be right about this being a suitable career for me. I mean to say, I did not find anything he had me do at all difficult. I might even consider it as a viable option, but I truly cannot countenance having to answer to John for the rest of my life. I have a suspicion Father knows this and is looking to oust me from my current state of indecision.

I am sure I would not mind finding a career for myself, but I haven't the faintest idea of what I should do. I am not clever enough for law, nor to be a professor. I'm sure I haven't the stomach to be a doctor, nor the proper gravity to be a vicar. And I know what you shall say: I have more than enough gravity. You take my meaning. I have not the soul of a vicar. Besides, vicars have to talk a great deal to people quite regularly and I'm sure I should hate that. Come to think of it, law poses the same problem. So does the medical profession. And teaching. Blast it. I wish I could be like you and Seb and simply look for a spouse. But the very notion of such a task fills me with utter dread. I want to retch just thinking about it.

My evenings at the club have been very strange lately. The manager keeps asking me if I would like to be introduced to people. Did she ever do that to you? I told her I knew no one in London, and then she said apparently some people would like to know me. This was a terrifying prospect, so I begged her to discourage them as politely as she could. She gave me an odd look but did as I asked. I have taken to practically inhaling my food in order to prevent this from happening again. I would take my meals at home but it is far too hot for such a thing.

If you were here, we could make a merry party of it at the club together. I'm sure you will tell me you have acquaintances in town and you would be perfectly happy to meet new people. Even if I were forced to suffer through some amount of society, it would be far less horrifying if I had someone to do it all with me.

Is there no chance I can persuade you to come stay in London?

Affectionately,
Gavin

FROM GERALDINE HARTFORD
Shulfield Hall, Tutting-on-Cress
TO GAVIN HARTFORD
8 Half Moon Street, London

10 September 1815

DEAR GAVIN,

I am not surprised to learn you have dispatched Papa's list so quickly. If it weren't for John, I'd say the career would suit you. But you would do much better to find something else. I know you said the idea of entering into the marriage mart fills you with dread, but I rather think you would do well at keeping house for someone. Far better than I will be, that's certain. You ought to stay for the Season when Mama and I return to London. Mama would be delighted as anything to find you a good match, and it was much easier meeting people with her around. I still don't see how you managed to avoid being pushed into marriage sooner. I suppose our parents sending you to London now may be an indication that your time is coming.

The manager at Nesbit's never approached me with such a message. Why on earth did you turn her down? I'm dying with curiosity as to who wanted to meet you. Whoever it was must have been very keen to go to the manager for an introduction. I hope your next letter tells me you went back and said you'd changed your mind.

I have already told you I have no interest in returning to London right now. Besides, we wouldn't have a chaperone. I suppose you are permitted to manage without one because you are there on business. Perhaps it is because you are so very careful all the time. Mama would have hysterics if she learned you and I were staying in the townhouse together with no one to keep an eye on us. I think you are correct that Papa may be giving you such responsibility in order to persuade you to get cracking. I'm sure he would be pleased if you took the opportunity to meet more people. Even without a chaperone, making new friends at the club cannot be objectionable.

I seem to remember advising you to be reckless in my last letter. I stand by this advice, if for no other reason than because I know perfectly well you will not heed it. You are, I think, too careful sometimes. What better time to challenge yourself than when you're in London?

Take heart. And do let the manager introduce you to people.

Affectionately,
Gerry

From John Hartford
   Lynnwood House, Sherton
To Gavin Hartford
   8 Half Moon Street, London

11 September 1815

Gav,

I was shocked to discover you were not in residence when Veronica and I arrived. Our father informs me that he sent you to London to look after the townhouse until the Season begins. He seems to think family steward will be a suitable occupation for you. Quite frankly, I can think of nothing less suitable. Although Father has directed me to keep such opinions to myself until you have had a chance to prove yourself.

Our mother says she encouraged you to stay in London for the whole time we are here. She claims there would be too many people at home. This is complete nonsense, of course. Geraldine is staying with our cousins and Sebastian is at Oxford. There is plenty of space. Besides, we will likely take up residence on the third floor. Particularly when the infant arrives. So there will always be a number of people in residence. Unless you intend to move out permanently. And that will be difficult until you reach your majority.

Father believes it will be good for you to live on your own for a while. However, Gav, I must admit to some concern about you being alone for so long. You are unaccustomed to it. We both know you have no talent for making decisions. If you do not desire to stay in London alone, and I will not be surprised if you don't, I will talk our parents into sending for you.

When you return, I would like to have a discussion with you. I feel you have dithered long enough on your plans for the future. It appears that neither of our parents has the least idea what will actually suit you. As the eldest, it is clearly incumbent to me.

John

FROM GAVIN HARTFORD
8 Half Moon Street, London
TO CHARLES KENTWORTHY, ESQUIRE
16 Berkeley Square, London

14 September 1815

MR. *KENTWORTHY*,

Please find enclosed what I owe you from last night's game of Vingt-Un. I know you will attempt to refuse it again.

But as I said last night, I am a gentleman, sir, and always honor my debts.

Gavin Hartford

FROM CHARLES KENTWORTHY, ESQ.
16 Berkeley Square, London
TO GAVIN HARTFORD
8 Half Moon Street, London

14 September 1815

MR. *HARTFORD*,

Do you always receive gifts in such a manner? As I told you last night, it was not a loan. When such a reserved young man allows himself the rare liberty to be the worse (or better) for wine, I hate to see him regret it. I had hoped removing any reasons for regret would encourage you to indulge more often. It would do you some good, in my opinion.

Besides, few people are as charming when they lose their inhibitions as you are.

Regards,
Charles Kentworthy

FROM GAVIN HARTFORD
8 Half Moon Street, London
TO CHARLES KENTWORTHY, ESQ.
16 Berkeley Square, London

14 September 1815

MR. KENTWORTHY,

Whatever you may think, I neither need nor want your charity. I have the funds. I was simply without them last night.

Nor do I want your opinion, particularly on what may or may not be good for me. I am perfectly capable of determining such things myself.

Nor was I in my cups, and I resent the implication.

G. Hartford

FROM CHARLES KENTWORTHY, ESQ.
16 Berkeley Square, London
TO GAVIN HARTFORD
8 Half Moon Street, London

15 September 1815

MR. HARTFORD,

I cannot imagine what I have done to offend, my dear, but please accept this copy of *Coleridge* as a peace offering. I seem to remember you saying your library was not as well stocked as you would like and how you had been searching for this volume. Considering your claim to have been thoroughly sober, you will undoubtedly remember the conversation.

Regards,
Charles Kentworthy

FROM GAVIN HARTFORD
8 Half Moon Street, London
TO GERALDINE HARTFORD
Shulfield Hall, Tutting-on-Cress

15 September 1815

GERRY,

You will never advise me to be reckless again.

With the townhouse so frightfully warm, I have continued to dine at Nesbit's Club. They keep enough spellcasters on staff to maintain cooling spells throughout the building and it is far more comfortable than what I can manage at home. However, as I detailed in my last letter, I've only been staying for short spurts before retreating back to the townhouse. I did not ask the manager for introductions, but I ended up meeting some of the other members despite myself.

You see, I went the other night in a fit of pique and got very drunk indeed. I am quite ashamed to admit it. It is very unlike me to get soused, as you well know. I can't say I recommend it or plan to try it again.

Some of the members invited me to join them in a game of Vingt-Un and I relaxed enough to do so, which is also unlike me. I was doing remarkably well, so naturally I kept playing. I then started to lose, as one sometimes does with card games. I wound up owing far more than what I had with me. Gerry, I have never had a gaming debt in my life. I don't understand what others see in it.

I was feeling pretty low about the whole thing when one of the other players came to my rescue. His name was Mr. Kentworthy and he paid my entire debt, which frankly made me feel even worse. It is one thing to be in debt to a club; it is another matter entirely for a complete stranger to pay you out. I tried to tell him not to. In fact, I think I got a little tetchy in my insistence. But the blasted man did not pay any heed to my arguments. I must have been drunker than I realized because all I remember is how well he tied his cravat and how perfectly his coat fit him.

Once I had properly sobered up, I sent him what I owed him. He replied by sending me a book I've been wanting. This is perfectly vexing as I do not recall having mentioned this book to him, but I can hardly admit that. It seems improper to accept it, but I dearly want to.

What's more, I was so embarrassed by the incident, I had intended to pay off my debt with him and end whatever association I'd made. And now we're conversing more than we had before. Far from ending my association with him, I seem to have started one. It is galling to have to ask for your advice, but I am positively flummoxed and you are the only person who will understand.

Affectionately,

Gavin

P.S. Much as it pains me to add this, I should confess that the whole incident happened because John wrote to me. Even the way he writes is irritating. He talks to me as if I am considerably younger than he is when I am, in fact, scarcely two years his junior. Just because he gained his majority sooner than we will does not make him magically more mature. He tried to persuade me to come home and said I am ill-suited to being alone in London. The thought of him knowing me better than I know myself put me in that fit of pique I mentioned at the beginning of my letter. John manages to vex me even from a distance. Odd how I was just complaining about wishing to go home and now I have absolutely no desire to do so.

Did you realize John and Veronica intend to take over the third floor of the house? I'm sure I didn't. I know he is entitled, and it really shouldn't surprise me, but, dash it all, I hoped marriage would keep him out of the family seat. I had no idea it would ensconce him more firmly into it. Our poor parents.

FROM GERALDINE HARTFORD
Shulfield Hall, Tutting-on-Cress
TO GAVIN HARTFORD
8 Half Moon Street, London

18 September 1815

DEAR GAVIN,

I did not know John and Veronica intended to take over the third floor, but I admit I am not surprised. John is far too thrifty to countenance leasing or buying another home out of consideration for our parents. You find it odd that a letter from John would make returning home less appealing, but I certainly do not need a letter from him to confirm this. I imagine they would have to travel about eventually to visit other people. I shall happily wait until they do so before returning home again, if I can manage such a thing. I have no desire whatsoever to share the same roof as Veronica.

Don't be a goose. Of course you should accept the book. And don't tell me you were rescued by Mr. Charles Kentworthy. I only know him by reputation. He is quite the rake, from what I understand. He's supposed to be very fashionable and possibly dangerous. But then that may just be an exaggeration. Dashing people are often considered dangerous by their very nature.

Everyone says he's one of the most eligible bachelors in London. I met many people who had tried to capture his attention, but I hear he is determined to stay single. Is it true he enjoys the company of both men and women? And yes, I'm being indelicate and don't you dare lecture me for it. I've never known someone to be of multiple persuasions, but I cannot determine if this is because we are from a small community or if it is truly rare. It is not the done thing, you know, to go about asking people of their persuasions, so I had to guess most of the time when I was in London. Is he really on friendly terms with Lord Byron and the Prince Regent? And is it true about those parties? I wish to know everything.

Affectionately,

Gerry

P.S. Please send me some fashion plates. The ones here are quite old and that will not do.

FROM GAVIN HARTFORD
8 Half Moon Street, London
TO CHARLES KENTWORTHY, ESQ.
16 Berkeley Square, London

20 September 1815

MR. KENTWORTHY,

I cannot think how you could have remembered my mentioning that book, but I cannot pretend I am not gratified that you did. I am sure I should reject such a gift, but I confess I am too pleased by it to do so.

I feel I must also apologize for being churlish. I am not accustomed to being so unguarded. It was decent of you to spot me the money, but I wish you hadn't needed to.

G. Hartford

• • •

FROM CHARLES KENTWORTHY, ESQ.
   16 Berkeley Square, London
TO GAVIN HARTFORD
   8 Half Moon Street, London

20 September 1815

MR. HARTFORD,

Keep the book, my dear. I insist. I remembered your mentioning it because I was surprised such a grave person would be interested in poetry.

I hope you will not mind if I confess I was pleased to have an opportunity to finally meet you. I've seen you dining at the club for the past fortnight and I have never in my life observed a quieter and more reclusive gentleman than yourself. My curiosity was piqued even further when I witnessed you indulging in what I can only presume to be a highly uncharacteristic mood.

In short, you intrigue me, darling. If you will forgive me for saying so.

I would never describe you as churlish, but I will accept your apology if you agree to join me in my box at the opera tonight. Please do me the honor of satisfying my insatiable desire to get to know you better. Lady and Lord Partridge will be there as well, lest you fear for your reputation.

Sincerely,
Charles Kentworthy

FROM GAVIN HARTFORD
   8 Half Moon Street, London
TO GERALDINE HARTFORD
   Shulfield Hall, Tutting-on-Cress

20 September 1815

GERRY,

I cannot imagine why you think I should be on such good terms with Mr. Kentworthy as to know all of that, and I am certainly not going to ask him. He does seem to be a pretty decent chap, however. He even invited me to join him in his opera box. I do not deserve this kindness as I'm sure I was perfectly horrid to him. I have not decided if I will accept. I shall have to mull it over.

I wish Mother had not insisted I stay in London alone like this. You know as well as I do I am no great shakes at making decisions by myself. I need you here to tell me what to do. It is quite selfish of you to not be around when needed.

Affectionately,
Gavin

FROM GAVIN HARTFORD
   8 Half Moon Street, London
TO CHARLES KENTWORTHY, ESQ.
   16 Berkeley Square, London

20 September 1815

MR. KENTWORTHY,

You are too kind, sir, and I regret to admit, far too generous with me. I daresay you will be quite underwhelmed upon further acquaintance. As alarming as I find it to pique the interest of any stranger, and as much as I fear I do not deserve such friendliness, I would hate to be boorish by rejecting your generous invitation. I shall be happy to join you.

G. Hartford

From Charles Kentworthy, Esq.
16 Berkeley Square, London
To Gavin Hartford
8 Half Moon Street, London

20 September 1815

Mr. Hartford,

My word, darling, do you always describe yourself in such an unkind manner? I can assure you I have no anticipation of being disappointed upon knowing you.

I am delighted that you should accept my invitation. I will come by your residence at seven to collect you and we can travel to the theater together. We shall dine with the Partridges after.

Until then,
Charles Kentworthy

From Geraldine Hartford
Shulfield Hall, Tutting-on-Cress
To Gavin Hartford,
8 Half Moon Street, London

23 September 1815

Dear Gavin,

The delay in learning such news is exasperating. Don't tell me you were such a clodpole as to refuse an invitation to Mr.

Kentworthy's opera box. I shall go quite spare if you do. You must tell me simply everything about it. How was the opera? Did he have a good box? What did you discuss? What does he look like?

Was it just the two of you in the opera box or were there others? You have never mentioned your persuasion, but if rumors about him are to be believed, it might be prudent to make sure you are not alone with him overmuch. And pray, don't compare me to John because of this advice. I trust your judgment to not do anything foolish, but London society can be very particular. I would hate for you to be punished for actually being sociable for once.

Have you forgotten about my request for fashion plates? I am reminding you in case you have.

Affectionately,
Gerry

FROM GAVIN HARTFORD
8 Half Moon Street, London
TO GERALDINE HARTFORD
Shulfield Hall, Tutting-on-Cress

26 September 1815

GERRY,

The opera was excellent. Mr. Kentworthy has his own box and the seats are remarkably close. I was able to get a wonderful view of the costumes, scenery, and spells. I believe I counted at least a half dozen spellcasters in the wings, performing all sorts of illusion spells and levitation spells. And they did it all so quickly I could barely see their work. I must say, the opera does a fine job in hiring such a talented crew. The experience was even more spectacular after understanding the work that went into it.

Mr. Kentworthy was kind enough to escort me to the theater himself. He came by in his own barouche so I did not have to walk about town or hire a hackney at all. On the way to the theater, he asked me if I had been to the opera before.

"Never," I said. "Although, I have heard opera music before. I mean, there were a number of people at home who sang, and I believe some of the songs were from operas."

"Did you enjoy it?"

"Very much. The music is breathtaking." I paused.

"And?" he said.

"Well," I said. "I must admit to some regrets that my Italian is not up to snuff. I always miss a great deal of the words that are said—that is, sung."

I felt very foolish for this confession, but he simply nodded and said, "That does certainly detract from the pleasure. I would be happy to offer some translations if it would help."

"Oh, Lord," I said. "You have no need to do that."

He laughed and said, "I would be only too glad to, darling. I have seen this performance before. I assure you, I would not offer if I minded."

As promised, he sat beside me in the theater to provide translations of key moments and answer any questions I had, which was jolly kind of him. He kept his arm around the back of my seat so he could more easily lean in with the occasional translation. His leg kept pressing against mine, which I found surprisingly intimate. I'm sure I should have pulled my leg away but I didn't quite dare.

I'm glad it was so dark in the theater for I must have been blushing profusely the entire time. I felt nervous at first with the close proximity and the prospect of asking him questions. But I found him remarkably easy to talk to so I gradually got more comfortable. He seemed delighted when I grew bold enough to offer my opinions. At one point I mentioned how strange it was that a character would be so certain of their interest.

"No one forms attachments so quickly," I said. "I'm sure I never do."

"Never?" he said.

"Well, he has only just met her, and already he is singing arias about her."

He did not reply, but he seemed to think it funny I should make such a remark. He often looked at me with an expression of amusement. Frankly, I do not understand it.

We went to the Royal Saloon for dinner afterwards. I am not accustomed to keeping such late hours, but—and I hope you will not think me stupid for saying so—it did make me feel oddly grown up. I have not really done anything in London since I arrived, besides dining at the club. It was an odd experience to be out and about with fashionable people at a fashionable time. No one would mistake me for fashionable, least of all you. So I daresay you will be surprised by it.

I'm not sure I believe your scandalous description of Mr. Kentworthy now that I have his acquaintance. You would think from his colorful reputation he would flirt with every person he met, but he was proper the entire time. He didn't even flirt with Lady Partridge and I believe she is supposed to be very beautiful. Other than some small talk with people who approached us, his attention was entirely directed at our party. Why, he barely even noticed other people for he remained focused on his conversation with me most of the evening. I daresay all the talk about him is just stuff.

The only detail that supports this reputation is his propensity to address others, including me, with terms of endearment. He called me everything from "my friend" to "darling" and "dear." It was a little shocking and terribly modern. But many people we met received something similar and they took this eccentricity as a matter of course. So I suppose I ought not to be so shocked by it. Are we dreadfully sheltered, Gerry?

We discussed all sorts of things at dinner. He was eager to hear my opinions of *Coleridge*—the book he gave me. He wanted to know my favorite poems and who my favorite poets were and why.

He asked about my family. I spoke of you and about how you were at Tutting-on-Cress now that the Season is over. I talked about Seb and all those ridiculous pranks of his. I told him about John and how I was sent away because he and Veronica had come to stay at home. I explained about all of the work Father is having me do. I talked about home an embarrassing amount, I'm afraid. I described practically everything about it to him. I daresay I am a little homesick. Can you believe it? After all my complaining about being at home all the time and now I should wish myself back.

Anyway, he listened to me prattle on, which was dashed civil of him. He asked a great many questions. Every time I attempted to curb my own sudden talkativeness, he would prod me to keep going. He would say, "What else?" "Tell me more," "And?" He seemed to always know when I was trying to hold myself back. I don't know if I've ever had anyone give me such focused attention for an entire evening. It was highly flattering, although it did make me disconcerted. I am unaccustomed to speaking so much to someone I barely know. In fact, I don't know if I've ever talked so much to anyone. And I have to admit, I enjoyed talking to someone who seemed genuinely interested in what I have to say.

Oh, and in answer to your previous query: Lady and Lord Partridge joined us in the box so it was all perfectly respectable. They joined us for dinner too, but they were barely at the table all night. They both kept leaving to talk to some acquaintance or other. So I have very little by way of description of them. They seemed quite nice, though.

That is, honestly, all there is to say about the evening. He had business in Bath and left this morning. We are to meet for luncheon when he returns, although I do not know when that will be.

Affectionately,
Gavin

FROM GERALDINE HARTFORD
Shulfield Hall, Tutting-on-Cress
TO GAVIN HARTFORD,
8 Half Moon Street, London

28 September 1815

DEAR GAVIN,

I notice you have omitted two topics of particular interest to me: my fashion plates and what Mr. Kentworthy looks like.

Also, my dear brother, you are a bit of a goose. Mr. Kentworthy does not need to flirt with everyone he meets to be a proper rake. I am particularly intrigued by your description of his tendency to use terms of affection. I've heard he spent a great deal of time on the Continent. Could that account for it? I regret to say it is possible we are very sheltered. I know I was quite surprised by how fashionable people behaved. Then again, I found it all rather exciting.

And you had best assure me you did not tell Mr. Kentworthy I was sent to Tutting-on-Cress because I had not managed to secure a husband. Imagine the most dashing man in London thinking I am unsuitable. It makes me want to scream. And if you were stupid enough to say such a thing, I insist you tell him as soon as he returns that this is not the case. If you do not, I will send you a curse. See if I don't.

Affectionately,
Gerry

•   •   •

FROM SEBASTIAN HARTFORD
Digory College, Oxford
TO GAVIN HARTFORD,
8 Half Moon Street, London

29 September 1815

WHAT HO, GAV!

I could not believe it when Father told me you were sent to stay in London. You get all the luck. Imagine being alone in London for months! I am stuck here at Oxford while you get to galavant around town. Father is always saying I am not responsible enough for such things. Do you know what I think? I think you ought to write to Father and have him send me there to stay with you. It would be capital! We would have such a jolly time! Well, I would have a jolly time. You would likely stay all day reading in the library or something. Truly, London is probably wasted on you. It is too unfair!

I played the most incredible prank last week. Stole a bust in the middle of the garden. What a laugh! The pedestal is empty and all of the faculty are scratching their heads. Best part is, the statue is there—only I've covered it with the most ingenious pair of spells, part invisibility and part levitation. So every time the dean swipes his hand over the pedestal, hoping to feel the stone statue, it is just air. Hilarious! Parks says it's my best yet.

Which reminds me, I owe Parks quite a bit for a gaming debt I've run up. Do you think you could see your way to lending me some money?

Anyway, hope London is a lark! Do try to do something interesting, if only for my sake. If I'm going to live vicariously through other people, the least they could do is have a good time.

Affectionately,
Seb

. . .

From Charles Kentworthy, Esq.
11 Royal Crescent, Bath
To Gavin Hartford
8 Half Moon Street, London

30 September 1815

Dear Mr. Hartford,

I hope London is keeping you entertained. If it is not, I hope you have enough poetry to keep you suitably occupied. And if you do not, I am enclosing a volume of Byron's poetry for you. Have you read him yet? I found this copy in Bath and thought of you.

I had hoped to conclude my business here within a week, but it looks as though I shall be forced to stay another week at least. I do apologize, my friend, for we shall have to delay our luncheon.

Charles Kentworthy

From Gavin Hartford
8 Half Moon Street, London
To Charles Kentworthy, Esq.
11 Royal Crescent, Bath

2 October 1815

Mr. Kentworthy,

You are far too generous with me, sir. I am sure I should not accept your gift. But I admit I will likely keep it anyway and hang the propriety.

You have perfect timing actually, as I have just finished reading every book of poetry our small library has to offer. I have resorted to reading books on magical theory instead and, while the subject is certainly interesting, I do not enjoy it half so well. Although, I have noted a few new spells I would like to try.

In any case, when I have exhausted poetry and magical theory, my next best option is to read my father's volumes on the history of the Roman Empire or a gothic novel that was undoubtedly purchased by my sister. After that, I can only find books on philosophy, etiquette, and sermons. I certainly have no desire to voluntarily be sermonized to, particularly when I am currently evading my brother's company. I suppose I could do worse than philosophy. At any rate, I greatly appreciate your gift. You are saving me from the Roman Empire, some sort of forest romance, etiquette, philosophy, and Fordyce.

With such a glowing report of what our library has to offer, I suppose I need hardly tell you I have found London to be perfectly dull since you left it. I daresay I am used to it by now. I have half a mind to visit my sister in Bedfordshire, but I do not think I would be welcome without providing a bundle of fashion plates for her. Can you countenance it? My sister has asked me three times now to send her some fashion plates. I'm sure I don't know where to find such things and which ones she might like. I have to tell you she is quite the cleverest person I know, but sometimes she is just as goose-witted as my brothers.

Pray do not hasten back on my account.

Gavin Hartford

P.S. I have been directed to clarify that the reason my sister was sent to stay with our cousins was not because she was too unsuitable to find a husband in London. She has threatened on pain of curse that I make sure you know this. I don't know why she thinks it important. Everyone who knows her adores her, as she must realize. Nobody would suggest she is actually unsuitable. Nevertheless, as I am failing in sending her fashion plates, I suppose the least I can do is ensure her name is clear with you.

I honestly cannot remember what I said about her at dinner. I fear I may have talked overmuch in general. I do apologize. I believe I must owe it to the fact that I drank a great deal of port. Why is it we meet under my most inebriated moments?

FROM GAVIN HARTFORD
8 Half Moon Street, London
TO SEBASTIAN HARTFORD
Digory College, Oxford

3 October 1815

SEB,

I am finding London to be rather dull, but I have to agree with Father in the matter of you coming here. You know perfectly well he will never permit you a jot of liberty if you persist in those stupid pranks of yours. Is it the influence of that Parks fellow? I daresay you ought to find better companions.

Ordinarily I would not give you a scrap of money. But as it happens, I recently ran up a bit of a gaming debt myself and someone was kind enough to assist. So I cannot, in good conscience, deny you the same generosity that was shown to me. However, I consider my experience to be an embarrassment and a serious lapse of good judgment and I have resolved never to repeat it. Do take care in applying the same lessons yourself, for I will not lend you money again.

Hope you are well.

Gavin

P.S. How many times must I ask you to stop calling me Gav? I've always hated being called that. I know I shall never get John to listen, but I should hope you might respect this request.

4 October 1815

DEAR MR. HARTFORD,

You are the first person I think of now when I see poetry. I shall continue to gift you with such volumes. You cannot stop me. And if doing so leads you to thank me for saving you from Fordyce, you can rest assured I will endeavor to save you from such a dire fate as much as possible.

I am curious about what spells have piqued your interest. I cannot claim any great talent for magic: my spells too often lack sufficient power. I make do with ensuring I employ talented spellcasters in my household staff, for I am no help in that department. Besides, I have little interest in theory so I have always been a poor student of the art. My friend Bertie has quite despaired of me. I'm sure if I were left alone in your library, I would read *The Romance of the Forest*—or any Radcliffe novel, for that matter—a hundred times before I cracked open a single book on magical theory.

I think you are the only person in London who finds it dull. You can hardly fault the city for it, darling. Why not venture out more? We are not yet into the Season, but there are still balls and parties to attend. If you would like to use my opera box, you are more than welcome to it.

Now that I think on it, I have never seen you anywhere around town except at Nesbit's. You are a handsome and intelligent young man. Surely you wish to meet more people and find yourself a spouse? You will certainly never accomplish such a thing if you stay at home or at the club all the time. Is it possible no one has shown you how to experience London properly? If this is so, please tell me at once and I shall make it my personal mission to instruct you.

While I would hate to advise you against visiting your sister, I must confess I will be greatly disappointed if you are not in town when I return. Please stay where you are, my friend, and I will conclude my business as quickly as may be so I can come back and show you how a person may enjoy London. I will even help you acquire the fashion plates for your sister.

Speaking of your sister, please assure her I was certain she is as beautiful and charming as her brother. London Seasons are fickle things and sometimes the most appealing of people go through a couple before finding a suitable match.

You most certainly did not talk overmuch at dinner. And I take exception to your apology when I put such work into getting you to talk at all. You are, I find, determined to be mysterious.

Sincerely,

Charles Kentworthy

P.S. Did your sister really threaten to curse you? She sounds positively hair-raising. I'm sad I missed the opportunity to meet her.

From Gavin Hartford
   8 Half Moon Street, London
To Geraldine Hartford
   Shulfield Hall, Tutting-on-Cress

6 October 1815

Gerry,

I will send you your dashed fashion plates as soon as Mr. Kentworthy returns. He has promised to help me pick out the wretched things for you. Why can you not write to the myriad people you met in London instead? Imagine sending your brother to shop for you. I daresay you never bully Seb or John like you do me. Shocking behavior in a sister.

Mr. Kentworthy told me to tell you he was certain you were, and I quote: "as beautiful and charming as her brother." He also told me plenty of people go through several Seasons without finding a suitable match. So do not fret on that account. I told him you had threatened to curse me and he said he wished he had met you, so I suppose he may be interested in courting you. However, I doubt Mother would approve of him, not with his reputation. Then again, I truly believe his reputation is mostly talk so perhaps Mother would relent eventually if she met him.

He sent me another book of poetry. I have never had a friend who shared my love of it before, besides Seb, and he is a younger brother so doesn't count. I feel as if I ought to give Mr. Kentworthy something in return, but I have no idea what. The man seems to have everything.

Speaking of Seb, I really do worry about him. You know Father will never trust him one bit with the way he carries on. I'm sure none of us were such goosewits when we were his age.

Affectionately,
Gavin

. . .

FROM SEBASTIAN HARTFORD
Digory College, Oxford
TO GAVIN HARTFORD
8 Half Moon Street, London

8 October 1815

WHAT HO, GAVIN!

Thanks ever so much for the loan! You really are a saint sometimes, do you know? Even if you won't let me come to London with you.

Who paid you out? I can't imagine you playing cards, let alone playing enough to run up a debt. London must be changing you. How thrilling! Maybe you'll even start smiling sometimes. Ha!

I wish you wouldn't be so sanctimonious about my friends. If it weren't for Parks, no one would talk to me. If you hadn't just loaned me money, I'd say you sound just like John.

Seb

FROM GERALDINE HARTFORD
Shulfield Hall, Tutting-on-Cress
TO GAVIN HARTFORD
8 Half Moon Street, London

9 October 1815

DEAR GAVIN,

What could I have possibly done to deserve such an addlepated brother? You were not supposed to tell Mr. Kentworthy I wanted him to know I was appealing, you dolt. You were supposed to casually slip it into the conversation. I am not attempting to win him as a suitor, but there is a world of difference between wanting to be courted by the most infamous rake in London and having that particular rake think of you as an unappealing spinster. Although I am sure you wouldn't understand such nuance. And do you mean to suggest you have determined the gentleman's persuasion? For you know I am dreadfully curious about it.

You have still failed to mention what he looks like.

I agree it would be good of you to give him a gift in return for his generosity. I cannot think of what would appeal. You know the man better than I. But I shall wrack my brain and try to come up with something.

Thank God he, at least, is unafraid of finding me some fashion plates. I confess I am even more impatient for them now. I should like to know what Mr. Kentworthy would pick out.

You're right about Seb. I don't know what happened when he went to Oxford because I don't think he was quite so foolish before. I blame his horrid friends.

Affectionately,

Gerry

P.S. I have enclosed a spell for you to try, however little I think you deserve it. It is one I created, and it is an extension of a standard fire spell. It prolongs the life of a candle, which seems uniquely helpful to your interests, particularly with all of those poetry books you seem to be acquiring. Do not try to cheat the spell and put a bunch of candles in the circle. It will work but it will be a weak spell on all of the candles involved. I advise you to use just the one and have it last a longer time. The spell can be recast using the same ingredients, but it will get weaker the more it is used. As it is a new spell, please send me whatever notes and observations you may have when using it. I need hardly tell you it is perfectly safe and has been tested by myself and the local spellmaster.

. . .

FROM GAVIN HARTFORD
8 Half Moon Street, London
TO CHARLES KENTWORTHY, ESQ.
11 Royal Crescent, Bath

12 October 1815

MR. KENTWORTHY,

I gratefully accept your offer to help me find some fashion plates for my sister. I'm afraid I owe her such a favor now, and having your assistance will be much appreciated. She just sent me a spell she built to extend candle life. I tested it last night and it was brilliant. I was able to burn a single candle for a good eight hours and it only went down an inch or so. She said it has recasting capabilities, but will get weaker the more often I use it. Is it selfish of me to wish she had sent me several packets of the same spell?

I am not sure I would go so far as to describe myself as any great talent in magic, but I am proficient. I lack suitable control, really, for I often overload my spells. But I do like the theory behind it all, to a degree. I can cast most spells, assuming they are of the Traditional variety. As soon as I am given anything particularly complicated—calculations or measurements or that sort of thing—I am quite lost. And I am certain Motion spellwork is beyond me. I have never tried it, but I suspect it is far more difficult than it looks. Magic usually is.

The spells I found in the books in our library are comfortably within my ability. I found a more powerful cooling spell. It has a smaller scope than the one I usually use, but it is more potent. It has been making my evenings in the library significantly more comfortable. There was also a cravat-tying spell that intrigued me. I confess I have little patience for having my cravat tied, so I look forward to speeding up the process. The cravat spell will require more practice, however. I nearly strangled myself with the first casting. Oh, and there was a spell I attempted for polishing my shoes—I thought it might be nice to take it off my valet's plate, as it were—but it was not particularly potent. Even with my tendency to overload power into it, it did little to my shoes.

I take some offense to your inference that I do not know the city properly. You talk as if I do not know how to enjoy myself. The truth is, I am restless no matter where I am. Every place quickly loses its appeal as I come to learn it. I find I have come to learn London and, thus, it has lost its appeal. I have no taste for gaming for obvious reasons. Like any country lad, I have a decent seat, but I dislike the idea of riding in the park. There are too many people about and they all seem very chatty. I would much prefer to stay at home. So I have. Thus, London is dull. Your offer to use your box is generous indeed, but it would not feel right to use the box without its owner. I shall wait for your return before I visit the opera again.

In answer to your question of marriage, I confess I am overwhelmed by the prospect. I have little interest in fatherhood, which complicates matters. As a secondborn sibling, I stand to inherit but little and, as such, am hardly a catch. I do not wish to prey upon heirs or heiresses to gain my fortune. Anyone in my family would hasten to tell you I tend to be a horrid grump; I could show you letters detailing me as such. With little fortune and a bad temper to boot, I have long given up the notion that I would be a desirable companion.

I am sure you will disagree with this assessment as you seem uniquely determined to think well of me. Nevertheless, I am attempting to resign myself to finding a career and settling alone somewhere in the country, preferably near my sister so I can beg her advice as much as I want and she can scold me as much as she wants. The trouble is, I cannot determine what career would suit. I am sure this is not a problem you have found yourself facing, but I will gratefully listen to any recommendations you might offer.

What a dreary topic that is. How is Bath? I have never been. I have a great-aunt, however, who took the waters and swears by it. I hear they cast some sort of spell on the water to give it healing properties and I have long wondered if it is true. Do you take the waters, Mr. Kentworthy?

G. Hartford

FROM CHARLES KENTWORTHY, ESQ.
11 Royal Crescent, Bath
TO GAVIN HARTFORD
8 Half Moon Street, London

15 October 1815

MY DEAR MR. HARTFORD,

My business in Bath is nearly concluded. I have not had occasion to take the waters. But if you are curious, I will gladly travel back with you to see your curiosity satisfied.

You may take offense to my criticism, but you are truly doing a poor job of experiencing all London has to offer. I promise to remedy that upon my return. I must warn you, however: you will have to talk to people in order to experience the city. I shall do everything I can to make sure this is not too painful for you. Prepare yourself, therefore, for rides in Hyde Park, dinner parties, balls, and races. I am determined to see you enjoy yourself. I trust you will pose a challenge, but I love a good challenge. And you shall soon learn, darling, that I always rise to the occasion.

It pains me that you speak of yourself as you do. If I am, as you say, uniquely determined to think well of you, then you are in an equal rage to think ill of yourself. It will not do, dear. I fear you dwell too much in your own head. I plan to keep you as busy as possible in the coming months to curb that habit. I expect filling your calendar will also resolve your other problem: your prospects for marriage. If you are not engaged within six months of our friendship, I will be very much surprised.

I hope you have not used that spell to its final sputterings. You never mentioned your sister was proficient in spell-building. If you can spare some of the castings until I return, I am curious to see it in action. Frankly, I am curious to see all of the spells you have described to me. Although I confess to some misgiving about any spell replacing a valet when it comes to cravat-tying. It is an art, my friend, and one well worth the patience.

By the time you receive this letter, I will be a few days behind it.

Sincerely,
Charles Kentworthy

FROM GAVIN HARTFORD
8 Half Moon Street, London
TO GERALDINE HARTFORD
Shulfield Hall, Tutting-on-Cress

18 October 1815

GERRY,

Thank you kindly for the spell. It is genius. I have already used it up. I was able to keep the same candle for over a week, despite using it every night for six or seven hours. The spell did not truly start to weaken until the twine began fraying. I did not interfere with whatever preparations you did for the ingredients, but I believe treating the twine to keep it from fraying would extend the spell's length. Can I persuade you to send me another? Mr. Kentworthy expressed an interest in seeing it in action.

Are you working on any other spells? Does Mother know you have apparently begun a career in spellmastery? God knows what she would think. I'm sure I don't mind having a sister in trade, but I daresay Mother would not approve of you doing something so decidedly beneath our station. I'm also given to understand that designing spells is rather dangerous. Should I be worried? You are my little sister, after all. Do give me some credit for brotherly concern.

What is Tutting-on-Cress like? I nearly came to visit you there, but Mr. Kentworthy urged me to stay in London until he returned. I suppose it is rude for me to tell you of my rejected plans to visit, but you sometimes threaten to curse me, so I call it even.

He returns to town soon. I am torn between being glad to see him again—for I have missed his conversation—and being wholly despairing of his arrival. Gerry, he has threatened to show me how to enjoy London. I am sure this sounds perfectly thrilling to you, but I know it to be a ghastly prospect. I shall have to ride in Hyde Park with him. And talk to people! I am wretched at the thought. I have a good mind to turn him down. But he has been so dashed good to me since the night he saved me at Nesbit's, it seems churlish to reject his offer. He must see me as frightfully lonely and isolated. If he simply supplied me with poetry and the occasional conversation, I would be perfectly satisfied. I suppose a man-about-town like him wouldn't understand. I imagine you will not understand either. More's the pity.

I am not at all sure what you wish to know about Mr. Kentworthy's looks. He is a tall man. I suppose you might call him athletic, for he has a good amount of muscle on his arms and shoulders. He cuts a dash in everything he wears. Ties a good cravat. You know I am no good at guessing ages, but I would believe him to be five or so years my senior—in his early thirties, perhaps, or thereabouts. He has large, brown, angular eyes and a large mouth that often appears to be smiling or turned up at the corners as if he is trying to hide a smile. This isn't to say his mouth or his eyes are large in an unappealing sense. Our family is somewhat plagued with small eyes and small mouths, so I tend to think his features are rather pleasing. Anyway, he has very nice teeth. His skin is more tan in color than ours, which doesn't take much; we are an absurdly pale lot of people. I don't mean to imply his skin is tan from the sun, but rather naturally a few shades darker than ours. His hair is dark. Not dark like mine, for mine is still red, you know. Or red in certain lights. I've often wondered how all four of us managed to have red hair. I know I'm the least gingery of us, but all the same. Is that normal, do you think? In any case, Mr. Kentworthy's hair is so dark as to be black. There. Does that satisfy you?

I believe I have already told you about how much I talked in his company. I have discovered his influence in this manner extends through correspondence as well. I found myself telling him all about my concerns about marriage, even going so far as to confess that I did not think anyone would find me suitable. This is something I have only told you, so it is a little shocking that I said so much to him upon so little acquaintance. I daresay I'm making a cake of myself.

What's worse is he has taken it into his head to find someone for me to marry. I am sure Father and Mother would be delighted that I have formed an acquaintance with someone determined to help me in such a way. But I shudder to think how he will see me when all of his lovely plans fall apart because I am not as eligible as he seems to think.

Hopefully my next letter will include fashion plates and you can stop pestering me on the subject. I intended to wait until he returned to reply to you, but I did not want to delay my request for more of your spells.

Affectionately,

Gavin

FROM JOHN HARTFORD
Lynnwood House, Sherton
TO GAVIN HARTFORD
8 Half Moon Street, London

19 October 1815

GAV,

I notice you have not yet replied to my letter. I must presume the postmaster has lost it. I hope you are not ignoring me. I am only seeking to help you.

It appears you intend to stay in London, imprudent though the choice may be. I suppose you had better make the most of it. I am sure you will receive this advice with your usual peevishness. You must understand I hoped to have this conversation in person.

The fact is, you have reached a marriageable age. I admit I was not married until I was six and twenty. You are now only five and twenty. But it will likely take you longer to find a wife than it took me. So you had better start looking now. I fear if you wait too long, you will simply never do it. I know you will argue with me, but I am convinced bachelorhood will ill suit you. It already ill suits you, frankly. Much better to get the whole marriage situation over with and start to settle down. Trust me.

If you do not marry, you will need to determine a suitable career. You have shown no inclination towards any occupation whatsoever. The longer you delay, the fewer options you will have. I need hardly tell you that I would certainly never turn you out, but I doubt you will want to live on my good graces alone. As I said in my previous letter, I do not think acting as steward on the family's behalf will satisfy you for long.

Veronica has drawn up a list of suitable young ladies who might already be in town. She offered to also draw up a list of suitable young men, but you have given no indication that you are of any particular persuasion. So we decided to assume your persuasion is the same as mine. If we are incorrect in this assumption, do tell me, and Veronica will send a list of gentlemen instead.

You will need introductions to these ladies, of course. For that you will need to socialize more. Veronica has drawn up another list of families in our acquaintance. These families will introduce you to the right sort of people. Both lists are included with this letter. Some of the families on the second list have members at our club. This will likely be the best way to start things.

Remember that you are in town without a chaperone, so take care you initiate these conversations when you are in the company of others. A person's reputation is a fragile thing and nextborns are particularly vulnerable. Veronica has also written to a few of the families asking them to invite you to dinner parties. Veronica has been very generous with her time on this matter. Remember to write her a letter thanking her for everything she is doing on your behalf.

Send me a report of how you are getting on and who you have met in London. It would have been better if I were there to assist you. You were sent to London prematurely and ill-equipped. You have never had a talent for talking to people. But needs must, Gav. You can no longer hide behind your usual timidity. Our parents appear to be unbothered by your reserved nature, but I must tell you no one likes talking to a wall. It is high time you outgrew that personality trait. This venture in London could decide your entire future. So, as I said before, we will have to make the most of it. I would have far more peace of mind if I knew you to be well settled.

I am sure you will gripe, for you are never satisfied with

anything. You must learn to recognize when people know better than you. I will certainly answer any questions or concerns you may have, but we both know you will not send any. You have always been too stubborn to simply ask for help.

John

FROM CHARLES KENTWORTHY, ESQ.
16 Berkeley Square, London
TO GAVIN HARTFORD
8 Half Moon Street, London

20 October 1815

DEAR MR. HARTFORD,

I am pleased to inform you I am back in London. I do not wish to presume you have a fully open social calendar, but if you are free today I will gladly come collect you for our lunch. I had thought Nesbit's would suit, unless you have opinions to the contrary.

I have drawn up some ideas for what I am calling your London education. I look forward to sharing them with you. If there is anything particular you would like to do, I will be only too happy to add it to the curriculum.

Charles Kentworthy

FROM GAVIN HARTFORD
8 Half Moon Street, London
TO CHARLES KENTWORTHY, ESQ.
16 Berkeley Square, London

20 October 1815

MR. KENTWORTHY,

Nesbit's will suit me perfectly well. I have been taking my meals there daily since I arrived in London and find the food quite satisfactory. What time do you usually luncheon? I should think I need hardly tell you I have no social obligations whatsoever at the moment. So I am at your disposal. I don't suppose there is any chance I shall be able to persuade you to give up this endeavor? I am living in dread of what a London education might entail.

I appreciate your consideration, but I have nothing particular in mind in terms of experiencing London. Except perhaps a good bookshop. My sister recommended Hatchard's, so I think I would like to go there. I confess I have not ventured out to find it myself as I was very worried I might get lost along the way. If you are familiar with the establishment, I would be grateful for your assistance. Perhaps when we collect my sister's fashion plates, you can direct me accordingly.

G. Hartford

From Charles Kentworthy, Esq.
  16 Berkeley Square, London
To Gavin Hartford
  8 Half Moon Street, London

20 October 1815

Dear Mr. Hartford,

I shall arrive at your door at half past two.

I am sorry, my dear, that you are living in dread of my plans. My intention is to offer you entertainment, not torture. As I said before, I am determined to see you enjoy yourself. Please do not fret about the impending education. I promise I shall be at your side every step of the way. I am certain you will capture the hearts of everyone you meet and will take London by storm. Just because you are blind to your own charms, darling, does not mean you do not possess them.

I concur with your sister's recommendation of Hatchard's and I would be delighted to offer myself as escort. As a matter of fact, I have a number of establishments I would like to take you to. After all, I could not possibly usher you into society without ensuring you had the proper wardrobe for such a task. So I look forward to the excuse to take you shopping.

I pray you will take heart in the face of these challenges; I have nothing but confidence in you.

Sincerely,
Charles Kentworthy

FROM GAVIN HARTFORD
   8 Half Moon Street, London
TO CHARLES KENTWORTHY, ESQ.
   16 Berkeley Square, London

21 October 1815

MR. KENTWORTHY,

I just received an invitation to a dinner party hosted by Viscount Finlington. I believe you are to blame for this. My brother has threatened that I shall be receiving invitations from his friends, but Finlington was not on the list of names he sent me, so this one cannot be his fault. Also, how the blazes did you procure an invitation for me when you only arrived in town yesterday?

   G. Hartford

FROM CHARLES KENTWORTHY, ESQ.
   16 Berkeley Square, London
TO GAVIN HARTFORD
   8 Half Moon Street, London

21 October 1815

DEAR MR. HARTFORD,

I work in strange and mysterious ways. It would not do for me to reveal all of my secrets.

Consider your education as a man-about-town underway.

As your guide through the pleasures of the city, I cannot allow you to proceed under my tutelage in anything less than a perfectly tied cravat. The one you sported yesterday was a travesty indeed. I am sending over a new cravat for you; kindly have your man starch and press it. I will arrive two hours before the dinner party to help you with the knot.

Charles Kentworthy

From Gavin Hartford
8 Half Moon Street, London
To Charles Kentworthy, Esq.
16 Berkeley Square, London

21 October 1815

Mr. Kentworthy,

I never agreed to being a man-about-town. Need I remind you that notion was all your own?

And I know how to tie a cravat, for God's sake. The knot I wore yesterday was done by the spell I told you about. I thought it a rather good attempt, considering. It was certainly more convenient than having my valet tie it for me and a good sight better than having to tie it myself. I don't see why you should wish to give me more work to do. You cannot possibly convince me you spend two hours on your cravat every day. If you tell me this, I shall pack up and go home this instant, horrid older brother notwithstanding.

G. Hartford

From Geraldine Hartford
Shulfield Hall, Tutting-on-Cress
To Gavin Hartford
8 Half Moon Street, London

22 October 1815

Dear Gavin,

I will send another candle spell when I have enhanced it. Thank you for your observations. I will see what I can do about the twine, but adding any more inflammatory items to the spell may counterbalance what is already included.

I have another spell I am fiddling with. I will send it to you when it is ready.

No, Mama does not know about my experiments in spell-building. I trust you to keep that to yourself. And don't fuss. I am being perfectly careful. Mr. Fenshaw, the local spellmaster, is teaching me a great deal. I promise not to be reckless.

It is fascinating, though. You know when you go into a spell shop and find all of the spell bags hanging on the walls? Mr. Fenshaw has been teaching me how those are constructed. A great deal of work goes into them. Some ingredients have to be measured first, or treated, or weighed. The spellmaster has to determine how much of each ingredient will be needed for a single casting, and whether the spell has recasting abilities. Each spell bag should contain sufficient materials for a single casting of the spell. Then, the spellmaster writes out a little instruction card detailing how to set up the spell, what the sigil looks like (if any), what the incantation is (if any), and instructions for deactivation. I have bought ever so many spell bags in the past, but it never occurred to me to think about the work involved. Magic is truly a fascinating science. I wish they taught it as such.

In terms of whether or not I have started a career in spell-mastery, let us relegate that to a later determination. I would adore being permitted to design my own spells and package them for people. Whether I will be permitted to do so other than as a hobby remains to be seen. As you so aptly pointed out, our parents are unlikely to permit such a step down in society. And if I were to take such a drastic step, it would probably damage your chances of a good match, not to mention Seb's. Really, the way Seb goes on at school, he may very well damage his own chances for marriage. I'm quite sure either you or I need to make a good match first. If you were to find a spouse sooner rather than later, Seb and I might have more room for maneuver. Even in that case, and if our parents approved my stepping down in such a way, I am past the proper age for apprenticeship. So it is likely all a lost cause.

Tutting-on-Cress is lovely. There are enough wealthy people who live nearby to account for well-stocked shops, which suits me perfectly. As it was at home, there is less call for perfection at all times than in London. I am able to be more myself without fear of ostracization. Everyone seemed to take it in stride when I began experimenting with spells. Such eccentricity would never be allowed in town.

I have made several friends here. I think you would like Julia Hearst best of all of them. She is a very sensible woman. You like sensible people, even when you aren't being one yourself. Before you start to protest: I am not attempting the role of matchmaker. Julia is very much in love with our cousin, Rose. I expect a proposal any day now. Like you, Rose takes a while to become comfortable with new things, so I suspect Julia of biding her time.

I would have enjoyed a visit, but I imagine Mr. Kentworthy will be better suited to entertain you. I am sure you will hate socializing at first, but I think it will do you good. Gamboling about London with Charles Kentworthy will be quite the experience and you should not pass it up for the world, no matter how uncomfortable it makes you at first. He seems to be the closest friend you have had since we were children—aside from me, of course. And while I love being your good friend, I do not think it can be healthy that your only friend be your little sister.

If anyone can find you a suitable match, I daresay it would be someone like Mr. Kentworthy. Having someone to offer introductions helps a great deal. I know I found it to be the case when I was in London, so do stop being so dismal about your own prospects.

Trust you to give me a description of my own family when

I'm asking for a description of somebody else. Why would I need to be told we are all redheads with pale skin? You really are a goosewit sometimes. I hope you get better at describing people. I intend to give you plenty of opportunity to practice as I wish to know simply everything about your adventures in London. I have never met Lady and Lord Partridge. What are they like?

Affectionately,
Gerry

FROM GAVIN HARTFORD
8 Half Moon Street, London
TO CHARLES KENTWORTHY, ESQ.
16 Berkeley Square, London

25 October 1815

KENTWORTHY,

You seemed interested in this book when we went to Hatchard's the other day, so I went back and bought it for you. You cannot expect your propensity for gifts to be entirely one-sided, can you?

G. *Hartford*

FROM CHARLES KENTWORTHY, ESQ.
16 Berkeley Square, London
TO GAVIN HARTFORD
8 Half Moon Street, London

25 October 1815

DEAREST HARTFORD,

What a darling you are, to be sure. Thank you kindly for the book.

I will see you tomorrow afternoon for the races. And don't fret your pretty head about being corrupted with gambling dens and horse races. You do not have the temperament of a gambler, so I introduce you to these vices with a clean conscience.

Charles Kentworthy

FROM GAVIN HARTFORD
8 Half Moon Street, London
TO GERALDINE HARTFORD
Shulfield Hall, Tutting-on-Cress

26 October 1815

GERRY,

First and foremost, here are the fashion plates. I hope to God they satisfy you. Kentworthy had it on good authority that these were the latest. He sends them with his compliments and had the cheek to suggest you repeat the request in a few months so he may have an excuse to drag me around the shopping district again. I had half a mind to omit that part, but I am sure either you or he would winkle it out of me if I did. You both have the uncanny ability of knowing when I am keeping something from you. How do I manage to surround myself with such people when I am, as a rule, a fairly private person?

Along with the fashion plates, I am sending you a book on magical theory. I was surprised to find a volume covering more than Traditional spellwork. From what I can see, it includes some modern examples as well. Kentworthy seemed to think finding fashion plates warranted a full day of shopping. We visited the ladies' shops for your request, but also went to a haberdasher, a tailor, a bookstore (he agreed with you on Hatchard's), and a spell shop. I found this book at Hatchard's and thought you might like it.

All in all, the shopping trip was rather pleasant. Although I own Kentworthy had me purchase far more than was strictly necessary. The man insisted I buy a great many new clothes: coats, waistcoats, shirts, cravats, cravat pins, hats, trousers, shoes. I am glad I have spent so little since coming to London, otherwise I'm sure I would have incurred Father's wrath. And Father is tolerably hard to anger really. Well, unless you're Seb.

I am also glad Kentworthy took me to the bookstore and the spell shop first. After the expense of the clothing, I doubt I would have been able to countenance buying myself books and spells. Frankly, I consider those items more of a necessity than additional clothing. I was able to stock up on some good volumes of poetry, which was nice, and replenished my own personal supply of useful spells. In the end, I was hard put to stop Kentworthy from paying for everything himself. It would have been the outside of enough to have a friend buy me a new wardrobe.

After your letter, I admit I looked at the spell shop in a new light. I kept imagining you being the one to fill the spell bags with ingredients. It really is a shame you cannot make a go of it; I am certain you would do well at such tasks. You are so very organized and thoughtful, not to mention you have remarkably good handwriting. Considering how much I always depend on the instruction card in a spell bag, I am sure having one with nice handwriting would be a very good thing. At any rate, I am glad you have had occasion to try your hand at spell-building, even if it is only as a temporary hobby. Perhaps we can find a way for you to keep at it even after you are married.

For all my grumbling about his determination to educate me, I will say this about Kentworthy: he is comprehensive in his planning. No sooner had he arrived in London, he procured an invitation for me to attend a dinner party. Viscount Finlington was the host and I admit I was a little intimidated by the gentleman. I fancy he may even have been flirting with me, although I generally believe that sort of attention to be impossible in my case. When he met me, he pronounced me to be as "adorably charming" as Kentworthy had described. Flustered by the attention, I said even less than I usually do. Not to mention I was a little alarmed to learn Kentworthy has been speaking of me to others. As for Kentworthy, he seemed to find the whole situation very amusing.

He was seated away from me at dinner, so I could not speak to him at all. Everyone seemed intrigued by my presence there. Kentworthy was the only person I knew so it was plain he told the host to invite me. I was asked all manner of questions about my family, where I was from, my birth order, how long I intended to stay in London, and how I had met Kentworthy. It was awful being subjected to so much inquisitiveness. I was so nervous I responded to all their queries with the briefest of answers. Thankfully, their curiosity only lasted through the fish course. After that, I think they all lost interest in me. To be fair, I lost interest in most of them.

I had an easier time of it when I was only obliged to talk to my dinner companion. I was paired with a Miss Lydia Cartright, who could talk of nothing but her expectations for next Season. She kept up a steady stream of conversation, which was a relief, but also rather tedious. After dinner, her mother came and talked to me, so I had to hear everything Miss Cartright had already said from her mother's perspective. Kentworthy laughed when I told him about it later. He said I was the only unmarried person he knew who would find one of the prettiest girls in London a dull dinner companion.

I do not understand what was lacking in my description of Kentworthy. I feel as though you are never satisfied with anything. I cannot think what else you might wish to know about him in terms of his looks.

As for Lady and Lord Partridge, I suppose you would call them a handsome couple. Lord Partridge is tall, slim, and blond. with pale skin similar to mine. Although he doesn't seem to blush as much as I do, which is a little irritating. He has small blue eyes, a small mouth, and a large nose. His wife is not as tall, not as slim, and has tawny-colored skin and large brown eyes. From what I have observed of them, she is a firstborn and the one with the actual title. They were not at the dinner party, which was unfortunate because I would have liked to see some familiar faces.

I am sure you will ask me to describe everyone who was at the dinner party for you, but I barely remember who was there. I can tell you Viscount Finlington is taller than I am, possibly about John's height. He is a round sort of man, pale, has light brown hair and, like Kentworthy, a mouth that seems inclined towards smiling. In general, he is of a cheerful disposition, I expect. Also, he has the most striking grey eyes. Overall, I would consider him to be a very handsome sort of person. Miss Cartright is short and...I don't know...shapely? Although less so than Lady Partridge. She has dark brown skin and large brown eyes and a full mouth. Now do tell me I have described people well enough for you. I cannot imagine what else you might wish to know.

Would you believe Kentworthy came to my house two hours before the dinner party to show me how to tie my cravat? You know I've never had much interest in fashion. My valet has quite despaired of me. I even found a spell for the purpose. I actually thought the spell quite handy—well, after I had practiced it a few times and was no longer in danger of choking myself with it—but Kentworthy rejected such an endeavor outright. He said tying a cravat is an art and every gentleman should not only employ a valet proficient in the task, but should also be up to the task himself. I own I never considered cravats to be so very important, but he was so firm on the subject I did not dare argue with him.

Having him tie my cravat was, in itself, quite an experience. First, he tried a few knots and had us both look at me in the mirror until he decided which suited me best. Then he made me learn to tie it myself.

I would only ever admit this to you, Gerry, but having him so close was a trifle unnerving. I've already told you how unsettling it was to sit next to him at the opera, but this was worse somehow. There were no distractions and his focus was entirely on me, so I'm sure he noticed how much I was blushing from the attention. Not to mention the way his fingers brushed against my skin was very distracting. When he applied himself to the task, I held my breath so long I was a little lightheaded by the time he finally proclaimed himself satisfied. He was so pleased when I managed to emulate his work, I did not mind the idea of applying myself more often. Is that not strange?

I believe I have already described his propensity to address most everyone with a variety of pet names. It was disconcerting at first, but now I barely notice it. It is strange, indeed, for when we are together, he will sometimes omit my name completely and get my attention by saying, "my dear, what do you think of this?" or something along those lines— and I answer! I never thought I should do such a thing to anyone outside of my family, but I suppose life works in mysterious ways.

We are to attend some horse races tomorrow. He assures me he will not turn me into an inveterate gambler or some such thing. Apparently I do not have the temperament. At least I have that to my credit.

He has only been back a week and we have already gone riding in the park five times. He means to make it a point of going out nearly every day. He was generous enough to tell me I could use any of his horses, as my horse is still in Sherton. He even told the stablemaster I was permitted to borrow a horse when he wasn't present. The man is far too generous with me sometimes.

Then again, he also wants me to try boxing at Muller's Saloon on Bond Street. I feel as though I am forever at odds between thinking he wishes to spoil me with his friendship and wishes to torture me at the same time.

When I protested to the boxing plan he said, "You look peakish, darling. I shudder to think what your sister would do to me if I sent her country-bred brother back to her looking pale and wan. No arguments now. Do as you're told or I will write to your sister myself."

I do not know what I have done to deserve this treatment. Please tell me you have not been in correspondence with Kentworthy. I dare not imagine the schemes you two would concoct for me. I have half a mind to suggest I take up fencing rather than boxing. But knowing him, he would simply add fencing on top of everything else and I am already far busier than I am accustomed to being.

I confess, however, that for the first time in a long time, I have felt neither bored nor restless. Of course I will not tell him this. It would make him far too smug. This is also the reason my reply to your letter is so delayed. I have been shockingly busy since he returned to town. I've barely had time to read.

Oh, and John sent me a list of suitable young ladies. He also sent me a list of families I ought to know and told me Veronica has sent letters to her friends requesting they invite me to dinners and such. I have already managed to evade two of these invitations. I have been so busy with Kentworthy I actually had a good excuse. I suppose I should count myself fortunate Kentworthy launched his campaign before John was able to begin his.

Affectionately,
Gavin

. . .

FROM GAVIN HARTFORD
8 Half Moon Street, London
TO CHARLES KENTWORTHY, ESQ.
16 Berkeley Square, London

27 October 1815

KENTWORTHY,

I think I shall have to bow out for our usual ride in the park today. I have not yet recovered from the boxing lesson. I did warn you I was no boxer, but I do apologize for having to cancel our appointment.

G.H.

FROM CHARLES KENTWORTHY, ESQ.
16 Berkeley Square, London
TO GAVIN HARTFORD,
8 Half Moon Street, London

27 October 1815

DARLING HARTFORD,

I refuse to accept your cancellation. I am sending over a tincture for you to use. If you apply it with a cooling spell, it will help to ease some of your pain. At the risk of seeing you glower at me and accuse me of heartlessness, I am coming over to your house within the hour. You had better be dressed by the time I arrive, including a well-tied cravat. Given our delayed start, I will accept a simple knot today, but do not expect such exceptions from me again.

Charles K.

. . .

FROM GAVIN HARTFORD
8 Half Moon Street, London
TO CHARLES KENTWORTHY, ESQ.
16 Berkeley Square, London

27 October 1815

KENTWORTHY,

You are indeed heartless, sir. I have half a mind to set Gerry on you.

G.H.

FROM CHARLES KENTWORTHY, ESQ.
16 Berkeley Square, London
TO GAVIN HARTFORD,
8 Half Moon Street, London

27 October 1815

She would be on my side, darling.
Charles K.

FROM GERALDINE HARTFORD
Shulfield Hall, Tutting-on-Cress
TO GAVIN HARTFORD,
8 Half Moon Street, London

29 October 1815

DEAR GAVIN,

Thank you! Thank you! A hundred times, thank you! For the fashion plates and for this wonderful book. It is already my favorite book I own and I've barely opened it.

The fashion plates are everything I had hoped for. I cannot wait to discuss them with Rose and see her blush at the daring cuts. It may comfort you to know that as sheltered as we are, sweet Rose is even more so. Fortunately, she has Julia and myself to rectify that. I am grateful you have Mr. Kentworthy to rectify it in you. I daresay you will have a rough time of it at first for he seems like a strict taskmaster in his initiative to show you around, but I do hope you will keep with it, dear. You have a tendency to withdraw into yourself when you do not have someone to push you along. Mr. Kentworthy must see this and I am glad there is someone in London who has your best interests at heart. No, I am not keeping correspondence with him. I only wish I was.

Please thank him on my behalf for his assistance with the fashion plates and assure him I will most certainly ask for more. Papa may well gape at the expense of your clothes, but you can be sure Mama will tell him such things are necessary for a time spent in London. My wardrobe cost an outrageous sum, for I was not allowed to wear the same dress twice the entire time I was there. Papa will likely count himself fortunate to have only one daughter to outfit in such a way. Besides, you have never been one for a costly wardrobe, so you cannot be considered to be abusing the privilege. Furthermore, I think you underestimate how glad our parents will be that you are doing anything in London. I suspect they will be relieved at the evidence that you are not merely idling away in the library.

I was very pleased by your comments on the spell shop and my own prospects to that end. I wish the rest of society was as tolerant as you are on the subject. I am grateful Mr. Fenshaw has been so encouraging. I feel sure that if he could, he would have offered me an apprenticeship or a position in his shop by now. We get on so famously. Ah, well. At least he is willing to show me what he can. Thankfully neither Aunt Lily nor Uncle Gregory seem to care what I do; they are even more indulgent than our parents. I suppose I should count myself lucky I have learned any of this at all. Don't mistake me—I do count myself extraordinarily lucky. I only wish it could last. It puts a rather grim tone over the whole thing to know marriage will likely require me to give it all up.

You ask if it is strange you should devote more attention to your cravat for Mr. Kentworthy's sake. I find it better put that you seek to please someone whose company you enjoy. But then, I know you to be a person of gentler heart than you realize.

I agree with his assessment that only you would find Lydia Cartright dull. She is one of the most fashionable people in London, and is largely considered one of the most beautiful women in the *ton*. Everyone was discussing what an upset she will cause when she makes her debut next year. As I understand it, Miss Cartright's father is in politics, so she is out and about more than what might be considered usual. She will surely be the incomparable of the Season. I only met her once—we talked when I went to tea at her aunt's house— but I found her to be perfectly charming, not to mention incredibly lovely. Did you not find her lovely, Gavin? I have often wondered why I have never heard you describe anyone as attractive, but I cannot tell if it is from lack of interest or if it is more of you being private about things. Goodness knows how you developed such a preference for privacy given our family.

Thank you for the descriptions of Viscount Finlington and Lady and Lord Partridge. I appreciate the description of Miss Cartright, despite having already met her. So do carry on with descriptions of people. I would certainly prefer too much information than too little.

I am excessively curious about how you get on in boxing. Please tell me everything. Thank goodness Mr. Kentworthy saved you from whatever horrid people John and Veronica saw fit to set on you.

You will never admit it, of course, but I can tell you are enjoying yourself in London at last. I am so very pleased to hear it. Send Mr. Kentworthy my compliments.

Missing you dearly,

Gerry

P.S. As it happens, Veronica sent a letter to me. It was full of her usual drivel. A great deal of nonsense about my having nothing to show for a London Season and how I need to apply myself to finding a husband. She even went so far as to tell me what aspects of my personality I ought to change: "Gentlemen do not admire frankness in a lady." Which is absurd, really, considering how she never refrains from giving everyone a piece of her mind. She even started to get waspish about Mama's ability to act as my chaperone and suggested that she herself might be better suited to escort me around London next year. Heaven forfend. I think I'd prefer to receive letters from John and that is saying something.

FROM GAVIN HARTFORD
  8 Half Moon Street, London
TO GERALDINE HARTFORD
  Shulfield Hall, Tutting-on-Cress

1 November 1815

GERRY,

You're quite welcome for the book. I looked through it a bit before sending it to you. I am curious to know your thoughts on the advanced spellwork and Motion spells. I find myself rather daunted by the latter. Is that foolish of me? It seems like something that will naturally draw attention to a person—you know, to be waving one's hands about in such a fashion—and I cringe at the very thought of it. I have always found spellcasting to be a somewhat private activity anyway.

At home, I am free to make mistakes or take my time without fear of judgment or comment. Besides, I usually use magic for added comfort rather than for any particular necessity. I imagine you will not agree with me on this topic as you have never been opposed to being the center of attention. Moreover, you are not afraid of mistakes. So perhaps this is simply another iteration of my usual fears and anxieties.

I am incredibly relieved you are pleased with the fashion plates. You are lucky I have formed a friendship with Kentworthy, you know. You might never have received them otherwise. Now, that is the last I shall speak of them until you bring up the subject again.

My condolences that you had to read a single line coming from Veronica's pen. Everyone adores you and your frankness. I find myself forever torn between thinking she and John deserve each other and wishing John had picked anyone else for a wife. She brings out the worst in him. In fact, I wouldn't be in the least bit surprised if she helped him write his horrid letters. Although he has gotten progressively worse since their marriage, so it is difficult to tell where her influence begins and ends.

Thank God you are finally satisfied with my descriptions. Pray do not ask me to tell you about all of the people I have met in the park. There are too many of them and I can barely keep them all straight. Thankfully, we see Lady and Lord Partridge most days and I have already provided you with a description of them. We also see Viscount Finlington when we are out and about. Although he is so popular we are often unable to speak to him for very long. But Kentworthy always makes a point of greeting the viscount, so I'm glad I've already met him.

As for Miss Cartright, you and Kentworthy seem to be equally mystified. I don't know why it should signify. I do find some people attractive, but I prefer to keep such opinions to myself. As you so aptly pointed out, given our family, it is highly difficult to maintain any level of privacy. If I were to indicate my preferences, I have no doubt that Mother, John, Seb, and you would have a thousand opinions on who I should pursue and then foist those people on me. Now I have to add Kentworthy to the list of nosy people in my life. It is a matter of self preservation. Father is the one person I excuse from this as I know he doesn't care a jot who I marry as long I choose someone respectable. I wish the rest of you would follow his example.

As it happens, I have no mind to marry anybody. I have often said I do not consider myself to have the temperament for marriage. If I were to get married, for instance, I should be expected to raise children. God only knows what sort of a father I would be. It hardly bears thinking of. I should vastly prefer to stay forever a bachelor. John says I am ill-suited to life as a bachelor, but I think he is wrong. As John is now expecting a child, it hardly matters anymore what I do. I am not inheriting the estate, nor have I ever had any interest to. The only downside to this future is I shall have to see everyone else get married and spread out across the country. Who knows where you, Seb, and even Kentworthy will wind up?

I suppose I must determine a suitable career for myself, but I do not know what I might do. I keep hoping Kentworthy will suggest something clever I haven't yet considered, but he appears set on pushing me into the marriage mart. Considering his reputation as a confirmed bachelor, it is odd that he should be so intent on my getting married. I confess I have seen no indication of his interest in anyone, leading me to hold strong to my notion that his reputation has been highly exaggerated. I would not be surprised if he truly was determined to stay single. However, why he cannot recognize my own desire to stay single I cannot understand.

You ask how I get along in boxing and I can tell you I get along very poorly. I keep telling Kentworthy I am no boxer, and yet he keeps making me go. I daresay something unto-ward will happen—I will lose my teeth or be knocked uncon-scious—and then he will regret bullying me in such a way.

Furthermore, I rather hate how much a person has to strip down before boxing. Do you know that I am expected to be shirtless? It is most unseemly. I do not enjoy having my scrawny and entirely unimpressive figure on display. I suspect Kentworthy is aware of my discomfort for when he does touch me, whether it be my back, arm, or shoulder, he always does so with a light hand. It is a trifle embarrassing. I feel fragile and foolish that he should take such care. Although I can't deny it is gratifying to have a friend who is observant of these things.

Surprisingly, I am growing accustomed to my rides in the park. Yesterday morning, I found myself looking forward to it and it was a sensation I was not altogether comfortable with. You know I am not an outdoorsman, nor do I crave society. Yet, the rides are so frequent as to be almost routine now. I know who it is I shall meet most of the time, and so I do not feel surprised by the chatter. In fact, the chatter has reduced to light pleasantries as we all see each other so often. I am accus-tomed to the pace Kentworthy sets so I am no longer sore following our rides. I will admit we are having pleasant weather in London and I am finding the fresh air comfortable. If you are secretly communicating with Kentworthy—as I do not entirely trust your assurances to the contrary—I beg you will not tell him about my change of heart in this matter as he is rather inclined to smugness when he is right about some-thing. Impertinent man.

I suppose you could say I am enjoying myself in London, after all. Add this to the list of things I will not tell Kentwor-thy. I regret to say this includes your compliments to him. If I surrender an inch, he will use it to bully me through anything else he pleases. You would not have me made miserable in such a way, would you?

Affectionately,
Gavin

FROM SEBASTIAN HARTFORD
Digory College, Oxford
TO GAVIN HARTFORD
8 Half Moon Street, London

2 November 1815

WHAT HO, GAVIN!

You know you never responded to my last letter. Is it because I compared you to John? I really didn't mean it.

Gerry told me you have recently become acquainted with Mr. Charles Kentworthy and I could not believe it. Is it true, Gavin? I hear he's the most handsome man in London, and wealthy and charming. Oh, do send for me so I may come to London and stay with you! I would adore meeting Mr. Kentworthy. I'm sure his charm and good looks are simply wasted on you for you never appreciate attractive people as much as I do. Please write to Father for me and persuade him to let me go. I promise I will never ask you for another tuppence if you do.

Affectionately,
Seb

FROM GERALDINE HARTFORD
Shulfield Hall, Tutting-on-Cress
TO GAVIN HARTFORD
8 Half Moon Street, London

4 November 1815

DEAR GAVIN,

It is just like you to wish broken teeth upon yourself merely to prove someone wrong.

I am working on another spell right now, but it is taking some doing. It is designed to heat things for a sustained length of time. I have never been satisfied with the brevity of quick heating spells and am determined to improve the process. This spell involves dragon's breath, which is difficult to work with. I have to wear gloves the whole time to keep myself from getting ill. I have scarcely had to work with dragon's breath before. Usually, they treat the flower before they dry it so the poison does not infect the spellcaster. Mr. Fenshaw, our local spellmaster, said he has had to get it untreated and treat it himself to make it safe for his customers. But if it is untreated, it is a little more potent, so I have been using his untreated supply and simply wearing gloves. Only imagine the care I have to put into it. I have already ruined one pair of gloves with this experiment.

Fortunately, everything is a little less expensive when one is not in town. Of course, one has to pay for things that are imported or travelling a great distance. Otherwise, I find London to increase the prices of nearly everything. It is highly impolite. At any rate, my spending money is going a great deal further than it did when I was in town. So at least I have some extra funds with which to buy myself another set of gloves. I also have plans to buy myself a new dress. Now that I have these fashion plates, I can request something modern. And Mama will not see it until I have worn it several times.

She is a wonderful mother in many ways and far less strict than some of the mamas I met in London, but the dear woman is not very forward-thinking when it comes to fashion.

I have been giving a lot of thought to your musings on spellcasting. I would like to try my hand at Motion spells, particularly now that I have this book. I agree that your reticence to learn them most likely stems from your shy nature. However, when one is truly proficient, they are not supposed to be particularly showy, but rather subtle and small gestures.

Since I've started learning with Mr. Fenshaw, I have lost the feeling of magic being a private sort of business, as I am always doing spells in his company. If I am experimenting at the house, Rose usually keeps me company. I remember you mentioned Mr. Kentworthy was interested in watching you cast one of my spells. When I do send it to you, I will be curious to learn whether you allow him to play audience to your work and how that feels for you.

As for your thoughts on marriage—I really do disagree with you on the subject. I am sure you would not be happy if you remained a bachelor, although I know you will not believe me. In saying this, I realize I am allying myself with John—I shudder to even think of it—but I suppose he cannot be wrong about everything all of the time. He is due to be correct occasionally, however rarely that may be.

You really ought to tell Mr. Kentworthy you are enjoying yourself. I am sure you are not making it easy for the poor man. Although, if he is getting to know you as well as I think he is, he might be able to tell.

Please tell me all about your adventures around town.

Affectionately,

Gerry

FROM GAVIN HARTFORD
8 Half Moon Street, London
TO SEBASTIAN HARTFORD
Digory College, Oxford

5 November 1815

SEB,

I will do no such thing. Yes, I have become acquainted with Mr. Kentworthy, but I refuse to spend my entire time in London keeping you out of trouble. To be honest, I'm fairly sure my being here without a chaperone is somewhat exceptional. I highly doubt I would be permitted to watch over you without someone else here. I am very sorry for it, but you will just have to wait to come to London when our parents are at liberty to escort you.

Affectionately,
Gavin

FROM REGINALD HARTFORD
Lynnwood House, Sherton
TO GAVIN HARTFORD
8 Half Moon Street, London

6 November 1815

GAVIN,

From what my solicitor has told me, you have been managing your new responsibilities as steward very well. If you have questions, do not hesitate to send them.

I was surprised by some of your recent expenses. I hope you do not intend to make a habit of such exorbitance. As you so rarely exceed your allowance, I am not overly concerned, yet.

I hope you are well.
Father

FROM GAVIN HARTFORD
   8 Half Moon Street, London
TO GERALDINE HARTFORD
   Shulfield Hall, Tutting-on-Cress

7 November 1815

GERRY,

You really ought to wear an apron or pinafore of some sort when you do spell work. If you truly plan to continue building your own spells, you would do well to invest in such necessities. I think a nice pair of gloves that are not formal gloves would also be a good investment. I am sure stains, burns, and cuts from various spellworks are generally frowned upon in a Lady of Quality. I will keep an eye out when I go shopping to see if anything will suit. Unless, of course, you are opposed to such an undertaking. In which case, please tell me and I shall spare myself the effort.

I have found myself in the unique position of tourist under Kentworthy's influence. He discovered yesterday during our ride in the park that I had not yet seen the Tower of London. He cancelled all of our plans, including boxing, thank heavens, and took me to see the Tower. We are to go to Somerset House tomorrow to look at the paintings there. I fear the excursion may well be wasted on me for I have no eye for art. But Kentworthy seems to think it vital that I experience everything.

I daresay you are correct that I ought to tell him how much I appreciate his efforts. I am sure it is very wrong of me to keep it to myself. But it is galling to be forever surrounded by people who are always correct about everything. I know you will not understand as you are one of those people. I am sure I do not make it easy for him. To be perfectly honest, Gerry, I'm very surprised he puts up with me at all. I know I'm not an enjoyable person to be around.

Affectionately,
Gavin

FROM CHARLES KENTWORTHY, ESQ.
   16 Berkeley Square, London
TO GAVIN HARTFORD
   8 Half Moon Street, London

8 November 1815

MY FRIEND,

There is to be a boxing match at the Daffy Club tonight. Would you care to accompany me? I think you might like the sport more if you see some professionals attempt it.

Charles K.

FROM GAVIN HARTFORD
   8 Half Moon Street, London
TO CHARLES KENTWORTHY, ESQ.
   16 Berkeley Square, London

8 November 1815

KENTWORTHY,

As long as I am not expected to participate in the fight, myself, I daresay I might as well experience everything you have to offer.

G.H.

· · ·

FROM CHARLES KENTWORTHY, ESQ.
   16 Berkeley Square, London
TO GAVIN HARTFORD
   8 Half Moon Street, London

8 November 1815

What a delightful prospect, darling.
Charles K.

FROM GAVIN HARTFORD
   8 Half Moon Street, London
TO REGINALD HARTFORD
   Lynnwood House, Sherton

9 November 1815

FATHER,

I do apologize for the recent expenses. I can assure you, I do not intend to spend so much again. Quite frankly, I was shocked that the shopping trip had reached such a sum.

I have not found any of the responsibilities particularly challenging, but I will send word if that changes.

Sincerely,
Gavin

FROM GERALDINE HARTFORD
Shulfield Hall, Tutting-on-Cress
TO GAVIN HARTFORD
8 Half Moon Street, London

10 November 1815

DEAR GAVIN,

I should be offended that you ask so little of my time in Tutting-on-Cress, but if I am honest, I will admit very little is happening here. You likely already suspect this which would explain your lack of curiosity. All the same, I wish you would pretend to be a little interested in how things are with me. We can both agree your time with Mr. Kentworthy is much more exciting than my time in the country, but can we not feign ignorance of this knowledge?

I like your idea of equipping myself with some proper outerwear. Do please keep an eye out for me when you go shopping. I will see what I can find at the shops in the village.

You keep complaining about boxing. Can you not tell Mr. Kentworthy you would prefer fencing? Must you be so stubborn and goosewitted?

I cannot believe you have been in London for over two months and have never been to the Tower or Somerset. You deserve to be made a tourist, brother. You should have been one long ago.

As to your thoughts on why Mr. Kentworthy puts up with you, I admit I have a pretty good guess. If you have not already come to this conclusion yourself, I will keep my thoughts to myself. At least, until I think you are ready. All I will say at present is if the gentleman did not like your company, he would not pursue it as often as he does.

I am beginning to wonder if his reputation as a confirmed bachelor is yet another aspect to his personality that has been ill-reported. I, for one, would not be surprised if he did announce an interest in marriage, after all.

Affectionately,
Gerry

From Charles Kentworthy, Esq.
  16 Berkeley Square, London
To Gavin Hartford
  8 Half Moon Street, London

11 November 1815

Dear Hartford,

It is a fine day and we have, for once, nothing planned for the afternoon. You have been a remarkably good sport about my handling of your education, so I shall reward you with a choice: what shall it be today, my dear? There is a race we can attend, we can go to Muller's saloon and box for a few rounds (you are doing much better than you think—you only want practice), we can shop. I am at your disposal.

Charles K.

From Gavin Hartford
  8 Half Moon Street, London
To Charles Kentworthy, Esq.
  16 Berkeley Square, London

11 November 1815

Kentworthy,

I do not think I would be opposed to a ride in the park, if you have a mind to it.

G.H.

. . .

FROM CHARLES KENTWORTHY, ESQ.
  16 Berkeley Square, London
TO GAVIN HARTFORD
  8 Half Moon Street, London

11 November 1815

DEAR HARTFORD,

I suspected you were secretly enjoying our rides. I am so glad to learn I was correct. I rather think you like routine and, despite yourself, you like the society too. Well, my dear, if it is a ride in the park you want, then a ride in the park you shall have. I shall leave here within the hour, unless you decide to send all sorts of notes feigning your displeasure.

Charles

FROM GAVIN HARTFORD
  8 Half Moon Street, London
TO CHARLES KENTWORTHY, ESQ.
  16 Berkeley Square, London

11 November 1815

KENTWORTHY,

I do not feign anything. I am wholly honest all of the time. I did not say I would enjoy a ride in the park. I said I would not mind it. It is an entirely different thing. You know there is a world of difference between the two. You further know I am at my happiest when I am in my library alone. I wish you would not be so smug. Did Gerry tell you all that dither about routine and society? Utterly shocking if she did. Upon my soul, I never knew a more disloyal sister.

G.H.

FROM CHARLES KENTWORTHY, ESQ.
16 Berkeley Square, London
TO GAVIN HARTFORD
8 Half Moon Street, London

11 November 1815

DEAR HARTFORD,

For shame, my dear. How can you abuse your sister so? I have yet to meet or correspond with her, much as I should like the pleasure. I was simply stating my own observations as to your preferences and your character.

But I did not realize you spoke of these things with her. Tell me, do you discuss me often in your correspondence with her? I am all curiosity, darling.

Charles

FROM GAVIN HARTFORD
8 Half Moon Street, London
TO CHARLES KENTWORTHY, ESQ.
16 Berkeley Square, London

11 November 1815

You are utterly impossible, sir. I regret saying anything at all. Do hurry up and get here. I have been ready this past quarter hour.

Gavin H.

From Gavin Hartford
    8 Half Moon Street, London
To Geraldine Hartford
    Shulfield Hall, Tutting-on-Cress

13 November 1815

Gerry,

Kentworthy took me to Astley's Royal Amphitheatre yesterday. I'm sure I saw nothing like it in my life. They did a reenactment of a battle (I forget which one; you know history was never my strong suit) and it was spectacular. Although it did make me more convinced than ever that the military is not the career for me. I am sure I should hate such exercises. Of course, the performance did not include the real danger of, well, getting killed in battle. It sounds perfectly dreadful. Did you go when you were in town? To Astley's, that is, not to battle.

We went shopping today. Please find enclosed a pair of gloves that should suit your needs. I believe they are usually used for gardening or something. You may need to treat them with a spell or two to safeguard them against burns and such, but I imagine you are up to such a task. I recall that being a particular hobby of yours, casting spells on articles of clothing and accessories. Come to think of it, I still have the scarf with the heating spell worked into it that you gave me a few Christmases ago. I didn't bring it with me to London, but I'm beginning to wish I had, if I am to stay here through the winter. Now that I consider the matter, I should not be in the least bit surprised you have developed such a keen interest in spell-building. You have always had the knack; you simply lacked more formal training.

I suppose I have been remiss in my duties as your brother. Very well, tell me how Tutting-on-Cress is treating you. I am sure you are filled to the brim with gossip or you would not bring it up. Has Julia proposed to our cousin yet? I believe you said the engagement was imminent.

No, I cannot tell Kentworthy I prefer fencing to boxing as he would simply add it to the list of things we must do. I believe I have already told you this.

Affectionately,

Gavin

P.S. I am completely mystified by your remarks about Kentworthy's likelihood of getting married. Have you heard anything on the subject? I cannot think what I might have said that would indicate a change in attitude on his part. From everything I have witnessed, his thoughts on marriage are wholly related to my own prospects. He has never spoken about himself. I think you must be mistaken. Unless you have heard information from a different source? Are there rumors circulating about him desiring a particular partner? If that is the case, please tell me what your source is. I should like to verify the veracity of it.

FROM GERALDINE HARTFORD
Shulfield Hall, Tutting-on-Cress
TO GAVIN HARTFORD
8 Half Moon Street, London

16 November 1815

DEAR GAVIN,

Thank you very much for the gloves. I believe they will suit my purposes admirably.

Do you know, I'd almost forgotten about all of those articles I bespelled when I was at home and in London. I am glad you reminded me for they really do make excellent gifts. Do you have any particular garment or accessory you would like sent to you for Christmas? And any particular spells you would like worked into them?

I liked the Amphitheatre well enough, but I was distracted worrying if the horses were happy with their situation. Did you wonder at that as well?

As for Tutting-on-Cress, no, Julia has not yet proposed to Rose. However, Julia and I have been playing matchmaker to a delightful lady, Miss Lizzy Worcester. She's very chattery and has the sweetest disposition. But as I said in my earlier letters, there really are precious few prospects around. Lizzy confided in me that she was of multiple persuasions and I was able to ask her more about what that is like, so I do not need you to ask Mr. Kentworthy about that after all. Although, I suppose his answer may differ from hers. So if you do ask him, I'm sure I should like to know what he says on the matter. Lizzy explained that she is attracted to people —whether they are masculine or feminine comes secondary. It was a fascinating conversation. Anyway, Julia and I have a mind to pair Lizzy up with a gentleman in town, Mr. Canterbury. He is a dour thing and he would not suit me at all. But Lizzy has said she thinks Mr. Canterbury has the loveliest eyes. According to Julia, Lizzy's exact words were: "Just like a basset hound!" Her comparison is rather apt. It has been extremely diverting to see how often we can force their paths to cross.

I will admit this gossip is not nearly as thrilling as the stories you have been able to share. But Tutting-on-Cress is not without entertainment, even if we have to create it ourselves.

My goodness, but my idle thoughts did put you in a tizzy. I have heard nothing specific about Mr. Kentworthy's prospects or inclination to marry. I was simply making an observation. Might I add that your interest in the matter is rather telling?

Do continue sending me details of your adventures.

Affectionately,
Gerry

FROM WINNIFRED HARTFORD
Lynnwood House, Sherton
TO GAVIN HARTFORD
8 Half Moon Street, London

17 November 1815

DEAR GAVIN,

I hope London is not as horrid as you thought it might be. Although I do wish you would tell me how you are settling there. We are all doing quite well here, but I am glad I arranged for you to go away, for there really are quite a lot of people at home now.

I am writing to ask about your plans for Christmas. Are you planning to come home, dear? I think it might be a fine idea if you went to visit Geraldine and our cousins in Bedfordshire. But, of course, you may do whatever you think is best.

Your father has asked that I include a list of additional things he would like you to take care of. He says you have been doing a marvelous job of everything so far. I'm pleased you're doing so well with the responsibility. I was sure you would.

He also tells me to assure you he is not angry with how much you've spent while in town. He understands that living in London is more expensive than living at home. I, for one, was pleased that so many of the bills were for clothing, rather than books. Some of your suits were getting a little worn, so I am relieved by the evidence that you invested in better ones.

I hope you are enjoying London. Try not to spend too much time in the library, dearest.

With love,
Mother

FROM GAVIN HARTFORD
   8 Half Moon Street, London
TO GERALDINE HARTFORD
   Shulfield Hall, Tutting-on-Cress

19 November 1815

GERRY,

I daresay it is a good thing I did not come to visit you after all, if such schemes are your idea of entertainment. Now that I think about it, Kentworthy has not seemed as inclined to find me a match as I had feared he would be. That is, he has not thrown me together with any particular people. I have not seen Miss Cartright since the dinner party. We have met with other unmarried people, but it has never felt like a pointed attempt to encourage me into matrimony. Perhaps it is because I have been intentionally quiet on the subject of my persuasion. All the more reason for me to continue being so if it is keeping him from matchmaking.

I have no idea what you could be insinuating about my interest in Kentworthy's marriage prospects. I am simply concerned about my friend's reputation. I do not like the idea of people spreading misinformation about him. That is all. Pray do not speculate further.

We dined with Viscount Finlington again the other night. This time, however, it was not at a dinner party but just the three of us. I daresay when I arrived in London a couple of months ago, I would never have dreamed of finding myself in such elegant company as those two gentlemen. I was not seated near him at the dinner party for my status is not so grand as that. So I have a much better impression of the gentleman after meeting him in a more intimate setting.

The first thing I should note is he and Kentworthy seem to be very good friends. They were as easy with each other as you and I. They not only address each other by first names, but use familiar forms of those names. I had not noticed it at the party, so I was a little surprised by it. I also observed that Finlington possesses the same tendency to use terms of endearment as Kentworthy. It made me wonder if Kentworthy was influenced by Finlington or if it was the other way around; or if, perhaps, they both learned the habit in the same place.

Once again, I was a little struck by Finlington's flirtatious nature. I wish I could say I was less flustered this time around, but I regret to admit I was just as tongue-tied as last time. I was not surprised Kentworthy found this amusing—for I'm beginning to believe amusement is his natural state—but I was a little dismayed to realize Finlington seemed just as amused. It wasn't until after I dropped my spoon into my soup (Finlington had remarked on the shape of my mouth, if you can countenance it) that he finally said, "You poor darling creature, I'm so sorry. Don't mind me, my sweet. I always say whatever pops into my head. Dreadfully bad habit." He didn't exactly stop his teasing, but it reduced somewhat.

One final note about Finlington is that I have never seen a Person of Quality use magic to the amount he does. I would almost describe it as showing off, but he performed magic almost as if it were second nature to him. I think I only saw him assemble a spell once, but he must have cast nearly a half dozen over the course of the evening. I know Motion spells are increasing in popularity, but I've never seen them done so effortlessly. It was most fascinating. I would have liked to ask him about it, but I couldn't work up the nerve. Did you ever meet him when you were in London?

I received a letter from Mother today and she said I might come back for Christmas, but also said it might be better if I visited you and our cousins instead. Can you believe it? My own mother could take or leave seeing me before the year is out. I have not decided what I will do. I have half a mind to stay in town and, thus, make a statement that I do not need her input on my plans. But that seems churlish and I am trying to cure myself of the habit. I shall keep you abreast of my plans in any case.

Affectionately,
Gavin

FROM GERALDINE HARTFORD
Shulfield Hall, Tutting-on-Cress
TO GAVIN HARTFORD
8 Half Moon Street, London

22 November 1815

DEAR GAVIN,

I have not had the pleasure of meeting Viscount Finlington, although I have heard of him. From what I understand, he runs in even higher social circles than Mr. Kentworthy. He is very fashionable and very well-regarded. Also, from what I hear, very eccentric in the way only the highest members of society can boast. I daresay you are quite fortunate to be counting him among your acquaintances. I have heard a great deal about his fashion sense, a little about his flirtatious nature, but nothing about his magical talents. I'm intrigued to hear the viscount appears to be skilled in Motion spells. I have been learning Motion spells myself and have found them to be unreliable. I wonder how he manages to cast them with such ease.

As for your plans for Christmas, I do not know if you have

a bad option. If you go home, you will be able to bring back whatever items or books you have missed from there. And you can see Seb and our parents, which I am sure would please you. Then again, you would have to put up with John and Veronica, which I would not wish upon anyone, least of all for Christmas. If Mr. Kentworthy is staying in town, he might have some delightful ideas for spending the holiday. I think you ought to ask him.

I would, of course, love it if you came to visit us here. Please let me know in advance, however, so I may warn Aunt Lily.

How is London now that the weather is getting cooler?

Affectionately,

Gerry

P.S. I have finished the other spell I told you about—the one with the heat. I would like you to try it but I am missing an ingredient for it. It needs dried dragon's breath to work properly and there is no more stock of it in the shop here. Shall I send it on without the dragon's breath or wait until I have more on hand?

FROM SEBASTIAN HARTFORD
   Digory College, Oxford
TO GAVIN HARTFORD
   8 Half Moon Street, London

23 November 1815

WHAT HO, GAVIN!

I just had the most cracking idea! Are you coming home for Christmas? If you are, you should invite Mr. Kentworthy to come too. I'm sure Christmas would be much more exciting if someone interesting were there. No offense.

Affectionately,

Seb

FROM JOHN HARTFORD
   Lynnwood House, Sherton
TO GAVIN HARTFORD
   8 Half Moon Street, London

23 November 1815

GAV,

I am extremely disappointed in you. You neglected to thank Veronica, as I asked you to do. What's more, you failed to accept any of the invitations sent to you this past month. Must you be so stubborn?

Veronica's friends all tell her you have been too busy to visit with them. This is utter nonsense, as we both know, Gav. You are completely incapable of making friends, much less keeping any. You have not had a single companion outside our family since you were a child. So it is impossible for you to be too busy. I am sure you are merely sitting in the library all of the time, talking to nobody.

You are not the oldest in the family. But it is still vital you ensure a secure future for yourself. Even more vital, really. Further dithering is a luxury you can ill afford. You must apply yourself to finding a decent career or a good spouse. Most of the ladies on the list Veronica wrote for you, which I trust you still have, are firstborn children and will be inheriting their own fortunes. So you would not need to find a career. Do you not understand we are trying to help?

John

FROM CHARLES KENTWORTHY, ESQ.
  16 Berkeley Square, London
TO GAVIN HARTFORD
  8 Half Moon Street, London

24 November 1815

DEAR HARTFORD,

I have plans for an adventure for us, my dear. Prepare yourself accordingly.

Charles

FROM GAVIN HARTFORD
  8 Half Moon Street, London
TO CHARLES KENTWORTHY, ESQ.
  16 Berkeley Square, London

24 November 1815

What an ominous missive. I hope you know you are perfectly dreadful.

G.H.

FROM CHARLES KENTWORTHY, ESQ.
  16 Berkeley Square, London
TO GAVIN HARTFORD
  8 Half Moon Street, London

24 November 1815

I'm keeping you on your toes, darling. You know you enjoy it. I can just imagine your mouth twitching in the way it does when you're trying to pretend you're not pleased.

Charles

FROM GAVIN HARTFORD
8 Half Moon Street, London
TO CHARLES KENTWORTHY, ESQ.
16 Berkeley Square, London

24 November 1815

I have no idea to what you could be referring. I shall have to school my features, I suppose.

G.H.

FROM CHARLES KENTWORTHY, ESQ.
16 Berkeley Square, London
TO GAVIN HARTFORD
8 Half Moon Street, London

24 November 1815

I wish you wouldn't.

Charles

FROM GAVIN HARTFORD
8 Half Moon Street, London
TO GERALDINE HARTFORD
Shulfield Hall, Tutting-on-Cress

25 November 1815

GERRY,

Seb sent a letter asking me to invite Kentworthy to come

home with me. Seb seems uniquely eager to meet him, which alarms me exceedingly. So naturally I don't intend to actually do it.

I am not sure of Kentworthy's plans, but I do believe I trespass on his generosity too much. I do not wish to burden him if he had hoped to leave town or if he has already made commitments. Besides, I made a complete cake of myself last night and I should hate to be an imposition on top of everything else.

I think I might visit home for Christmas. In fact, I have almost made up my mind to do so. I'm sure John will be thoroughly unpleasant, as usual. Even his letters put me in a foul mood. Do you know, I think I may stop reading the blasted things. Seeing him in person will be far worse than reading his letters, but at least Mother and Father will be there, which should help somewhat. I do wish to see them and Seb, and there are a few things I would like to bring back to London with me. So I think I will brave the punishment that is our older brother in order to see everyone else and come back better prepared for an extended stay in town. Let me know if there is anything you wish to have sent to you.   ·

I would very much like a bespelled garment or accessory for Christmas. I will leave the options up to you, for you are far more creative than I. Although I will say a garment that repels water or absorbs it for drying purposes might come in handy—I shall explain shortly.

Kentworthy took me to Covent Garden yesterday. He had already taken me to the opera, but this time we went to a play.

After the play was over, he helped me put my coat back on and said, "I believe tonight the foyer will look a little different than it did the last time we came here."

"That is hardly an eloquent description," I said.

"Well, are you in an adventurous spirit, darling?"

As I'm sure you know, I never am, so all I could say was, "Oh, all right. Do your worst."

He grinned and led me downstairs to the foyer. I thought I knew what to expect since we had already gone to that district for the opera. But either I was too disconcerted by Kentworthy's company the first night to notice or it was a distinctly different atmosphere, for I can tell you I stopped in my tracks at the sight. The foyer was full of people. Most of the people were clearly patrons of the theater, and a good many of the people were vendors of some sort or other. But the rest were—well, I simply do not know how to put this delicately, Gerry—but I do believe the rest of the people were soliciting.

I probably looked discomfited because Kentworthy put a hand on my shoulder and said, "We'll pass through it quickly, all right?"

I nodded. He steered me through the crowd, keeping his hand on my shoulder the entire time. I began to think we would make it through without intervention when we were hailed by someone in the crowd. A young man greeted Kentworthy like an old friend, which was surprising, and wove through the throng to reach us. He kissed Kentworthy most scandalously—in public, if you please!—before Kentworthy introduced us.

"My dear," he said to me, "this is a friend of mine, Mr. Angelino Bowles. Lino, darling, allow me to introduce Mr. Gavin Hartford."

Mr. Bowles glanced between us before looking me up and down and giving a little mock bow. "Any friend of Mr. Kentworthy's…"

I nodded, feeling stiff and awkward under his scrutiny. "A pleasure."

Mr. Bowles sauntered forward and cupped my cheek with his hand. I was terrified by the prospect that he might actually kiss me, too. Some of my alarm must have shown on my face, for he immediately dropped his hand. "You're not afraid of me, are you? First time?"

"Not at all," I stammered. "That is, yes. That is—" I looked at Kentworthy, hoping he might intervene.

"I'm afraid we're not looking for that tonight, Lino," he said, placing his hand back on my shoulder. "I'm just showing Mr. Hartford around the London scene."

"Do you mean to say I'm not a part of the London scene, sir?" Mr. Bowles said with a grin.

"Oh, my dear, you are a decided attraction of it," Kentworthy said, returning the smile. "But, you see, my friend here is of a particularly reserved nature. I do not wish to make the dear man uncomfortable."

I had no idea what to say. I very much wanted to suggest we continue our way outside, but I hated to look a coward. Moreover, I had no idea of the protocol in such situations. Would I offend Mr. Bowles if I declared a lack of interest?

Mr. Bowles glanced between us again and said, "Perhaps your friend and I can talk for a moment, sir?"

Kentworthy did not immediately agree to this suggestion. I'm afraid some of my anxiety must have shown on my face because he looked quite concerned. I wanted very much for him to lead me outside immediately, but I also dreaded what he would think of my cowardice, so I nodded in assent before he had an opportunity to say anything.

"Certainly," I added, just to be safe.

Mr. Bowles walked me a little ways away. Kentworthy was, thankfully, still in view, but he turned so as to give us some privacy. Mr. Bowles returned to his previous stance in front of me. He had stunning dark eyes that were both intense and somehow knowing. He made me feel nervous with the way he looked at me. I was also a little distracted by how long his eyelashes were. I couldn't bring myself to meet his gaze, so I looked away. Then I was distracted by the way he wore his shirt completely unbuttoned, leaving his chest in full view.

Once again, he cupped my cheek—I fancied he kept his touch light for my comfort—and leaned forward to talk to me in a low voice. "What has you so spooked, eh? Nervous about your first time?"

I shook my head. "It isn't that, Mr. Bowles. Although, I can't deny that is also true." I felt my face flush at the confession.

He chuckled and said, "Just Lino, please." He rubbed his thumb slowly across my cheek as if to soothe me, like I was a skittish horse or something, and spoke gently, "I promise I won't hurt you. I think I'd like to try to make you smile a little. Are you always so grave? It can't be good for your health, you know."

I had no idea what to say to that, so I said nothing.

"What is it then? Prefer a lady? I can recommend some who will treat you gentle-like."

I felt utterly foolish that he should be so careful with me. I glanced over his shoulder at Kentworthy, suddenly worried he would overhear our conversation and be disappointed by my behavior.

Mr. Bowles turned a little to follow my gaze and then swiveled back to face me. "Ah," he said. "Perhaps our friend missed his mark by bringing you through here tonight. Is that it?"

"I'm sorry," I said at last. "I'm sure you think me a complete idiot. But I couldn't possibly—I do not like to be open about my persuasion, you see."

"Oh, I think I have a good guess," he said with a small smile.

"I really couldn't—" I went on, trying to ignore his comment. "But it is certainly nothing personal. I mean to say, you're very—" I broke off, feeling my face get hot. I was getting dreadfully flustered. "I'm sorry," I said again. "I'm afraid I'm not at all comfortable with the notion of intimacy with a stranger."

Mr. Bowles cocked his head, looking at me consideringly. "Nothing wrong with that, my pretty buck. Plenty of others are similar."

I looked up in surprise. "They are?"

He smiled. "Surely. But are you certain there isn't more troubling you? Maybe I can help? You know, jealousy can be very effective sometimes. Did you ever think of that?"

"I'm sure I don't know what you're talking about," I sputtered.

He laughed and brought his other hand up so he was framing my face. "Then again, maybe not. You're a skittery little thing, aren't you? I quite like you. So I'm going to give you some advice, all right?"

I nodded, tentative.

"I think you know what you want, but you'll never get it if you aren't willing to risk a little. Be bold, my pretty buck. Can you do that? Can you be bold?"

I was too disconcerted by his keen gaze to comment on the absurdity of his statement. So instead I swallowed and said, "Past experience would suggest I cannot."

He grinned and tilted my face up toward his. "Now, now, that's not the way. You can do better than that. I want you to surprise yourself tonight. Order a different type of wine or something," he said with a laugh. "Anything, but do something unusual. And try not to be so serious and frightened about it. It's adorable, of course, but you want to keep the fellow over there on his toes, don't you? It's good to keep them guessing."

He gave me a wink and then turned my face and planted a kiss on my cheek. Then he slung his arm around my shoulders and walked me back to Kentworthy. "You were right, sir. He's not ready for any of us yet. But I think he might be ready for dinner," he said. "And maybe get him some wine. He's too serious by half and I want you to work on that."

Kentworthy laughed. "Very good. You know best, Lino, as usual."

"That I do, sir," he said. With an arm still over my shoulders, he leaned forward and smacked another kiss on Kentworthy's mouth before swooping to kiss my cheek again. "Remember what I said, now," he said in my ear, and then he gave me a little shove towards Kentworthy and strolled off.

Kentworthy must have taken his advice to heart, for he took me straight to dinner. I regret to say my interaction with Mr. Bowles put me in a terrible muddle. I thought fiercely about it all through dinner, trying to think what on earth I could do that would be surprising. And since Kentworthy was the one who ordered for us, I couldn't even take Mr. Bowles's easy suggestion by ordering a different sort of wine. I felt as though the man had challenged me in some way and I had no idea what to do about it. Moreover, he had admonished me for being too serious and too frightened and I felt as if I was simply proving his point.

I fancy the whole thing made Kentworthy a trifle uncomfortable too, for he looked at me with a considering expression all through dinner. It put me ill at ease. This is all I have by way of explanation for my subsequent behavior, which is to say: I got very drunk indeed. It is highly embarrassing how I keep managing to do that in Kentworthy's company. Kentworthy's humor seemed to improve the more I drank, which is how I can best explain why I kept drinking.

"Didn't you tell me you had plans for an adventure tonight?" I said as we finished our dinner.

"I did," he said. "But I'm not altogether sure we should keep to my original plan. Is there anywhere particular you'd like to go?"

"Dashed if I know," I said. "You're the ruddy guide, aren't

you? There must be something else in London I have to see. There's always something."

"Perhaps we should—"

"I know!" I said, cutting him off. "Let us go to the Peerless Pond. You said we should wait until spring, but we can at least see it now, can't we?"

He smiled. "Why not? It's a mild night."

I know I have complained about Kentworthy making a tourist of me, but I confess I have actually been keen to see the pond. I am sure swimming in a large pool in the middle of the city amidst strangers would not have the same appeal as swimming in the lake back at home, but I do miss swimming. Peerless Pond was completely empty of people, of course. It was closed for the season, but Kentworthy bribed the guard to let us in to look. It was an unusually warm night for November and the wine I had been drinking made me warmer still. The moon shone through the trees and onto the still water. It was very inviting. I was struck with a sudden idea. Mr. Bowles had said to surprise myself, hadn't he? I began to unbutton my coat and loosen my cravat as we walked around the pool.

"Shall we go for a swim?" I asked Kentworthy.

"Not tonight, I think," he said, glancing across the water. "It is too cold."

I scoffed. "Stuff." I stripped off my coat and cravat and toed off my shoes.

"My dear," Kentworthy said, approaching me. "You cannot be serious."

I lifted my chin. "I am always serious. Don't you know?" I unbuttoned my waistcoat. "Mr. Bowles certainly seemed to think so."

"Is that what has you in this strange mood? What did he say to you, darling?"

I yanked off my waistcoat. "Well, come on!"

Then, I jumped into the pool.

Good God, Gerry, but it was abominably freezing in that water. I'm a tolerable swimmer, but the shock of the cold caused me to take longer to surface than I otherwise might have done. I had been too impatient (and, I'm ashamed to admit, too drunk) to strip off my trousers and they made swimming a good deal more challenging than I had anticipated. I heard Kentworthy yelling for me as I made my way up to the surface. I coughed and sputtered when my head came back up and swam back to the edge.

"God's teeth," I said. "It's bloody freezing."

"Of course it is, you ridiculous man," Kentworthy said, sounding strained.

He grabbed my arm and practically hauled me out of the water. I only barely registered him putting my coat around my shoulders and rubbing my arms through the fabric.

"You'll catch your death," he muttered.

"Nonsense," I said, my teeth chattering. "Used to go swimming all the time back at home."

"Oh yes?" he said, not pausing in his ministrations. "At this time of year?"

I tried to recall if I ever had, but my mind wouldn't focus for me.

Kentworthy, meanwhile, finally decided he had done the best he could in terms of drying me with my coat. He picked up my wrinkled cravat and began, to my utter horror, to dry my hair with it.

"What are you doing?" I said, trying to wriggle away from him.

He grabbed my arm and continued to work, one-handed. He did not answer me.

"We could really use a quick drying spell right now," I quipped, trying to distract myself from this indignity. "It's a shame they aren't safe to use directly on the body. I must ask Gerry to make one." Then I sneezed.

He stopped attempting to dry my hair. He pulled off his

own coat and wrapped it around me. Then he scooped up my shoes and my waistcoat, put an arm tightly around my shoulders and walked us both to the road to hail a hackney.

I sneezed again as we got into it.

He did not relax his hold on me, even after we had settled into the seat and he had given the driver my address.

"What caused you to be so impetuous?" he said quietly, as we rattled down the street.

"Isn't impetuousness...impetu...isn't one generally impetuous for no reason?"

"Not you," he answered. "You always have a reason."

When I turned to answer him, I was suddenly unnerved by his closeness. I shivered. "You ordered the wine," I muttered, looking away and pulling both coats closer around me. Sobriety was beginning to tickle the corners of my brain.

"Not saying I mind it. I would just like to know what set you off. Was it something Lino said?"

I sneezed again which, thankfully, seemed to excuse me from answering. He did not pursue the topic.

I am now, as you can well imagine, heartily embarrassed and most ashamed of myself. Imagine me getting so drunk I jumped into the Peerless Pond at the end of November. I can hardly countenance it myself and I was there. At any rate, I am paying severely for it now. I have the worst headache of my life and I am sore everywhere, not to mention outrageously tired.

I believe I can acquire some dragon's breath, so please send on the spell to me as is.

Affectionately,

Gavin

P.S. It is utterly stupid of course, but a small part of me wishes to go back to Mr. Bowles and tell him all about it. I'm not at all sure if what I did was precisely what he had in mind, though.

P.P.S. I realize I mentioned such a thing when I was intoxicated, but there really ought to be a quick drying spell that is safe to use directly on one's person. All the ones I've ever seen can only be used on clothes or items. Too many volatile ingredients, I suppose. Although you would certainly know better than I. I have no idea what you have planned in terms of spell experimentation, but I do ask you to bend your mind to the matter. Not that I expect to do such an idiotic thing again, of course. The same goes for the garment I mentioned above that can repel or absorb water. I should certainly hope I don't make a habit of such nonsense, but if I really am to stay in London long-term, it would be good to have items about my person to make the rainy season more comfortable.

FROM GERALDINE HARTFORD
  Shulfield Hall, Tutting-on-Cress
TO GAVIN HARTFORD
  8 Half Moon Street, London

28 November 1815

DEAR GAVIN,

Jumping into the Peerless Pond at this time of year was not, admittedly, your best moment. But you are so rarely reckless I can't entirely condemn it. Assuming, of course, you did not get a chill. I do hope you have recovered.

I like your suggestion of the quick drying spell, and the garment for such use as you describe. I shall, as you requested, bend my mind to the matter.

Also, from the sounds of it, Mr. Bowles would probably enjoy hearing an account of your evening. I rather think you should go back and tell him. You offered very little by way of a description of him and I must admit some curiosity as to what the man looked like. I suppose I am unlikely to form an acquaintance with him myself, if I am correctly understanding his occupation. I should also point out that he gave you some excellent advice, however recklessly you acted upon it.

I rather like your idea of not opening John's letters. They serve no purpose other than to put you in a foul temper, so you would be doing yourself a favor by ignoring them. If he truly has news for you, I'm sure Mama or Papa will send it on to you as well. Or I will. It will be good for you to ignore his advice and, I daresay, good for him to be ignored.

Sometimes you are a bit of a pinhead. Seb is clearly angling to meet Mr. Kentworthy because our little brother is the most determined flirt to ever walk on two legs. Furthermore, he will likely have heard how charming, wealthy, and eligible Mr. Kentworthy is. Seb's no fool, much as he might occasionally act like one. He is the youngest, so I am sure it has not escaped his notice that finding a good spouse is as important for him as it is for us. By the sounds of it, he is taking a much more active hand in the matter than either of us have.

I am enclosing the spell bag, minus the dried dragon's breath. You should be able to get it at a spell shop. Make sure you get some that is treated, for it can be dangerous to work with otherwise. The spell will not be as convenient to your particular interests as the last one, but I think you will find it interesting all the same. It is a heating spell, designed for small surfaces. I recommend using a small handkerchief or a rag for the focus. After you have cast the spell, you can use the focused object either over or under something you wish to keep warm. This can include: a plate or bowl, a cup of tea, hands or feet. Be careful if using it on your hands or feet as it may be very warm to the touch. I have been getting a great deal of use out of the spell by using it for my tea. As before, please send any observations or notes you may obtain.

Affectionately,
Gerry

. . .

FROM GAVIN HARTFORD
   8 Half Moon Street, London
TO WINNIFRED HARTFORD
   Lynnwood House, Sherton

1 December 1815

MOTHER,

I am sorry I have been remiss in telling you about my time in London. I can assure you I have been doing a great many things outside of the library. I have given the matter a good deal of thought and have decided to come home for Christmas. I would very much like to see you, Father, and Seb. It will be nice to tell you about how I am getting on in town. I imagine I will leave again shortly after the holiday and spend the new year in London.

   Affectionately,
   Gavin

FROM GAVIN HARTFORD
   8 Half Moon Street, London
TO SEBASTIAN HARTFORD
   Digory College, Oxford

1 December 1815

SEB,

Don't be an idiot. I will do no such thing. I am sure Kentworthy has his own plans and I have no desire to impose on him. But I am coming home for Christmas. I look forward to seeing you, even if you are more interested in meeting my friend than seeing me, you callous little sod.

Affectionately,
Gavin

FROM GAVIN HARTFORD
   8 Half Moon Street, London
TO CHARLES KENTWORTHY, ESQ.
   16 Berkeley Square, London

2 December 1815

KENTWORTHY,

I have just received another spell from my sister. Would you like to join me for dinner and then to observe the casting? I would invite you sooner, but I must purchase an additional ingredient first. Of course, if you wish to join me as I go to shop for it, you are welcome. I should warn you, however, that I am not entirely certain how long the search will take me. Gerry had some difficulty acquiring dragon's breath and I do not know if it is hard to get or if the small village shop simply had low stock.

G. H.

FROM CHARLES KENTWORTHY, ESQ.
   16 Berkeley Square, London
TO GAVIN HARTFORD
   8 Half Moon Street, London

2 December 1815

DEAR HARTFORD,

I gladly accept your invitation to dinner and to the casting. I wish I could join you as you shop, for you know how much I enjoy it. However, I regret to say I have an appointment today and will not be free in time to leave with you. If you have a mind to go shopping again tomorrow, I spotted a charming watch fob at Goring's shop that I am sure I must have. I almost bought it when I was there last week but talked myself out of the purchase, which I have since come to regret.

Charles

FROM GAVIN HARTFORD
8 Half Moon Street, London
TO GERALDINE HARTFORD
Shulfield Hall, Tutting-on-Cress

3 December 1815

GERRY,

I finally purchased a proper gift for Kentworthy. It was a dashed nuisance getting it, I can tell you. I purchased it while I was looking for the dragon's breath. I started with your recommendation to try a spell shop, so I went to the one Kentworthy took me to, but the spellmaster didn't have any. He said there had been a drought and many of the usual suppliers were out of stock. He advised me to try another spellshop, and gave me the address, which was dashed civil of him, but it was also quite out of my way.

I stopped to get my gift for Kentworthy. He mentioned in a note to me that he had considered buying himself a watch fob but had talked himself out of purchasing it and had come to regret it. He told me this by way of asking if I would like to join him as he went shopping the following day. It seemed too perfect an opportunity, so I went to the shop he referenced after I left the first spell shop. The shop owner kept trying to sell all manner of trinkets to me. I had a devil of a time getting him to stop. I finally got him to understand I was looking for a specific fob, one Mr. Kentworthy had considered buying.

When he realized what I was on about, he procured the fob readily enough.

Kentworthy told me he had found the watch fob to be "charming" but I found it to be almost understated. It was gold with a stamp inlay of a small branch with flowers on it. The ribbon was pale blue, which seemed to me an odd shade of color to pick as it may not match every outfit. But then again, he certainly knows more about these things than I do. I wasn't sure if I ought to get him a watch to go with it and the shop owner assured me most customers buy both. I daresay he merely wanted to get more money out of me, but I hated the idea of looking a fool by giving Kentworthy a fob and no watch to put on it. It was set at a shocking price, but I had already made up my mind to get it. So I bought the whole thing: the fob and a gold watch to match.

The whole time I rode from Goring's to the second spell shop, I justified the purchase in my head, mostly by thinking how much Kentworthy deserved my thanks. I'm stubborn, I complain heartily all of the time, and I can be downright churlish. Kentworthy has accepted all of this in good humor. He has listened to me griping and harping on and on about whatever inane thought I happen to have. He has taken me all over town in an effort to entertain me and push me to enjoy myself. He has been so patient and civil from the very first time I met him. I do not think I have been a good friend in return. Anyway, I kept going around and around in my head about how little I deserved Kentworthy's friendship and, indeed, anyone's friendship.

Naturally, this method of justifying my purchase did not put me in a particularly good mood. I was so distracted with my thoughts, I got quite turned around in trying to locate the second spell shop. It was a very seedy part of town, near the docks, and I spent a good hour wandering about looking for it. I finally had to stop and ask for directions. Fortunately, I got there eventually and the spellmaster did have what I was looking for. I purchased enough for two castings, just in case, and left.

No sooner had I left the shop when it started to pour. I was drenched within a block of the shop. The second time in a week in which I have been completely soaked to the skin while fully dressed. At least I was sober this time. I had half a mind to turn back and wait the storm out, but I was already soaked and I did not know how long the storm would last. My errands had taken me later and farther than I had originally intended. I had invited Kentworthy to dinner and to observe the casting, and after all of my miserable thoughts about my unworthiness, I was determined to not make myself an even worse friend by being late on top of everything else.

I'm sure I looked a fright when I finally arrived at home. My valet tried to convince me to take a bath, but it was close to the time Kentworthy had said he would arrive, so I waved off my valet's concerns and simply changed clothes and allowed for a cursory toweling off of my hair. I believe Kentworthy did the sensible thing and waited the storm out because he has not yet arrived and I have managed to write this entire letter while waiting for him. Perhaps I ought to have taken a bath after all.

Ah, I believe Kentworthy is here now. I will finish this letter in the morning and let you know how the casting goes. I would finish it tonight, but I am already completely exhausted and it will take all of my energy to be a good host. I daresay Kentworthy would recommend delaying the casting if he knew how tired I was, but after all I went through, I am determined to perform it tonight.

WELL, KENTWORTHY HAD WAITED THE STORM OUT, SO HE LOOKED neat as a pin, as usual. Blast him.

"Dinner is not ready yet," I told him. "Would you like to start with the casting while we wait?"

"I would be delighted," he said. "Don't tell me you got caught in the rain, my dear."

I nodded. "Got caught on the east side of town. Seediest little section. You wouldn't believe. I was looking for the final ingredient for the spell. It was dashed hard to locate."

"Why, in heaven's name, did you not wait it out?"

"I did not want to be late and keep you waiting. My errands had run later than I anticipated and I was much farther from home than I had planned to be."

He touched fingertips to my damp hair and said, "Good heavens, darling, you did not need to ride hell for leather for my sake."

"It is of no consequence," I assured him. "I was soaked within moments, so waiting would have afforded me little comfort."

"We can delay the casting, if you would like. I can come around tomorrow."

"Not at all. I rode all over town for this confounded spell. I'll be dashed if I don't do it tonight."

He tucked his hand under my elbow as we walked into the drawing room. "Very well," he said. "Tell me what this spell is for."

"It is a heating spell. Gerry says it will heat up plates and bowls and cups and that sort of thing."

"How fortunate. I'm sure you could do with a cup of tea right now. Shall I ring for it?"

"Not at all. Take a seat, if you please. I'll ring for the tea."

He smiled in that amused way of his and sat down. I rang for tea and set up the spell while we waited for it to be brought out. I was ready to cast the spell just as the tea tray came in. Kentworthy suggested I hold off on the casting until I had a cup of tea first. But I rejected such a foolish notion.

The casting did not go well. I'm not sure what went wrong. I followed all of your instructions as I usually do. But the hand-kerchief went up in flames in the middle of the casting, so I think I must have put too much power into it. Control has always been a challenge for me when it comes to magic, as you well know.

I was so startled I simply sat and stared until Kentworthy pulled me back by my arm and stamped the fire out. I believe he ruined his shoes too, which is horrible to think of. I truly am the worst possible friend to him. I'm glad I bought the spare dragon's breath, for I will have to cast it again. I am sorry, Gerry. You will have to send me another packet after you've received this. Obviously, after setting the focus on fire, the spell did not take as it ought to have done, so I have no notes for you except you ought to indicate how much power the spellcaster should infuse into the spell. I'm sure that would have helped me.

Dinner was ready shortly after we finished the casting, which was just as well as I was no longer feeling the thing. I started to feel progressively worse through dinner. I think Kentworthy must have noticed, for he took charge of the conversation and kept a steady stream of talk while I ate. He did not comment on my behavior until dinner was finished.

"Are you all right, my dear?" he asked.

"Just a little tired," I said. "I will be fine."

"Let us get you to a fire," he said, tucking his hand around my elbow again. "I do not wish for you to catch a chill."

He tried to coddle me then, insisting I sit closest to the fire and allow him to pour me a glass of port. I did not allow either of these things. In hindsight, this might have been a bit pigheaded of me. But my concerns over my own wretched personality were still fresh in my mind and I was determined to improve myself. So I made him sit on the sofa and poured the port myself. I made a point of asking him about his day and for any news he had of himself. I'm ashamed to say he was a little surprised by the direction in which I drove the conversation, but he put up little fuss.

"Have some port, Gavin," he said.

"Yes, yes," I said, and poured myself a glass. I sat back in my chair and then realized what he said. I gawked at him. "You called me by my name," I said.

His mouth quirked in a half smile. "I do believe I did."

"Strange," I said, feeling drowsy. "You never call me that."

"Do you mind?"

I shook my head and then regretted doing so. It made me frightfully dizzy. I groaned a little, closed my eyes, and leaned back against the seat. I felt Kentworthy's hand on my forehead. I opened my eyes to see him standing over me, brushing my hair away from my face.

"You ought to go to bed, my dear," he said softly.

I frowned at him. "You were in such a rage for me to drink a moment ago."

His hand came away from my face and rested on my shoulder. "You are perfectly correct, of course," he said. "Drink your port and then we shall see about getting you into bed."

I didn't even finish it before he took the glass away and rang for the butler. I honestly don't even remember the port. It just felt like it took forever to drink it. Nor do I remember seeing Kentworthy to the door. It wasn't until I was in bed that I realized I hadn't given him the watch fob.

Good God, Gerry, but I feel awful. I am sending this letter off to you now so it can be done, and then I am going back to bed. I woke up this morning and thought if I could just force myself to get up and do something then I might feel better, but I only feel worse after writing this. I have the most dreadful headache. I still feel dizzy. Every part of my body is tired and aching. Even with a cheery fire in the hearth, I am positively freezing. I am sure you would tease me for being so slothful, but all I can think of is crawling back under my covers and sleeping.

I suppose I ought not to have allowed myself to become soaked twice in one week. It is hardly surprising I feel ill, now that I think about it. I have obviously caught a chill and have no one to blame but my own stupidly stubborn self.

Affectionately,
Gavin

FROM GERALDINE HARTFORD
Shulfield Hall, Tutting-on-Cress
TO GAVIN HARTFORD
8 Half Moon Street, London

6 December 1815

DEAR GAVIN,

Good gracious, you do not sound well at all. If you do not write to me immediately with enough details to convince me you are better, I will travel to London at once.

Affectionately,
Gerry

FROM GAVIN HARTFORD
8 Half Moon Street, London
TO GERALDINE HARTFORD
Shulfield Hall, Tutting-on-Cress

9 December 1815

DEAR GERRY,

For heaven's sake, do not lose your head. I am perfectly fine. If you travel all the way to London alone, I will never forgive you. Neither will Mother, so stop fussing. It is simply a slight fever or something, nothing to fret about. Kentworthy is writing this while I dictate to him, which will explain the difference in penmanship and will also explain the "dear" at the beginning of the letter. He insisted.

Kentworthy has set his doctor on me. I am still feeling weary and my brain is still in a bit of a fog. I am suffering from some chills and a headache. The dizziness has subsided some, but is still strong enough to be a bother. Kentworthy says I should stop supplying you with details of my illness or else I will worry you. You really needn't come. I am being taken care of, much to my chagrin.

Affectionately,
Gavin

Miss Hartford,

I hope you will forgive my impertinence in addressing you directly when we have not yet been introduced. This is Charles Kentworthy.

Lest you think your brother is resorting to his usual tricks of downplaying a situation, I wish to assure you that he appears to be out of danger. I have brought my personal physician to see to him. I would not entrust Mr. Hartford's health to anyone but the best.

He was getting agitated at the thought of you worrying about him and I persuaded him to let me write the letter at his dictation. For some people, writing can be a restful experience; I have noticed this is not the case with your brother. He pours a great deal of energy into the task. I do not think energy is something he ought to expend freely at this moment, as it will not help him to improve any faster.

I will not be so bold as to discourage you from traveling here, although I fear such a journey may not be safe for a nextborn alone. I can assure you your brother will not be left by himself while he is ill. When the doctor is unavailable to sit with him, then I will. I give you my word I will inform you if his condition worsens. If it improves, I daresay he will inform you of it himself. As it is, he is glowering at me for writing so much without his dictation.

Your servant,
Charles Kentworthy

FROM GERALDINE HARTFORD
Shulfield Hall, Tutting-on-Cress
TO GAVIN HARTFORD
8 Half Moon Street, London

12 December 1815

DEAR GAVIN,

It is just like you to think you are not sick when you are, in fact, exceedingly ill. It would account, in part, to the overall moodiness in your previous letter. I have a great many thoughts on this subject that I will keep to myself until you are well enough to discuss them, except to say: don't be such a ninnyhammer, Gavin. For goodness's sake. Do you think I would enjoy your company if you were the person you described? I'd like to think you appreciate my intelligence enough to know I would not suffer such a boor. I am never one to discourage introspection, but I find you do it more than is healthy. I do urge you to be kinder in your own estimation.

When you are recovered, we will discuss the contents of your previous letter at length. In the meantime, I hope you feel better soon. Do not worry about the spell. I will send you another when you have improved so you can do a proper casting.

Affectionately,

Gerry

MR. KENTWORTHY,

I will gladly forgive your impertinence if you will forgive mine in replying to you. I wish to thank you for putting my mind at ease and add an even greater thanks for seeing to Gavin's wellbeing. I feel greatly relieved knowing you are there to take care of him.

Do you think he will be well enough to go home for Christmas? You see, my parents are expecting him. If you do not think he should be moved yet, I will write to my mother and warn her that Gavin will not be coming home as planned.

Sincerely,
Geraldine Hartford

FROM CHARLES KENTWORTHY, ESQ.
8 Half Moon Street, London
TO GERALDINE HARTFORD
Shulfield Hall, Tutting-on-Cress

15 December 1815

MISS HARTFORD,

I do not think your brother will be well enough to travel at this juncture. It might be best if you told your parents not to expect him. I'm afraid he has lapsed back into a fever, but I do not think there is as yet any reason for alarm. The doctor has prescribed laudanum and I am making your brother take it. He needs rest most of all, which will explain this letter without his dictation preceding it. I will continue to inform you of any developments to his condition.

Your servant,
Charles Kentworthy

. . .

FROM GERALDINE HARTFORD
Shulfield Hall, Tutting-on-Cress
TO MR. CHARLES KENTWORTHY, ESQ. ℅ GAVIN HARTFORD
8 Half Moon Street, London

17 December 1815

MR. KENTWORTHY,

Thank you again for taking care of poor Gavin. I have told my mother of the change in plans and I suspect she will be on her way to you as soon as she gets my letter. She is a solicitous person by nature, particularly regarding her children. In fact, she sent Gavin to London out of concern that he might be bullied by our older brother. Although my father pretended the reason was so Gavin could learn to take care of property, and Gavin is determined to believe the real reason he was sent away was because he was a nuisance. Which, quite honestly, tells you as much about Gavin's character as it does about my parents and my brother John.

I would come see him myself, despite the dangers of traveling alone, but I do not think having more people fussing at him will improve Gavin's health. He has never enjoyed being the center of attention, even when he feels perfectly well, and I would hate to make him uncomfortable—well, more uncomfortable than he already is. If I am wrong, however, please tell me, and I shall come to assist you in any way I can.

Sincerely,

Geraldine Hartford

P.S. Please inform Gavin, if he is well enough to hear it, that Veronica and John had their baby, a boy, and everyone is doing well, according to my mother.

. . .

From Charles Kentworthy, Esq.
  8 Half Moon Street, London
To Geraldine Hartford
  Shulfield Hall, Tutting-on-Cress

19 December 1815

Miss Hartford,

I do not wish to cause you alarm, but I must admit to some concern over your brother's condition. He has been ill for over a fortnight now and shows no sign of improvement. Thankfully, he does not exactly get worse, but he still has a fever. He sleeps only when he is given laudanum. Even then, his sleep does not appear to be restful as he is ever tossing and turning. He complains frequently of the headache and of chills, but his skin is clammy and flushed. If your mother is coming to London, then I can wait upon her opinion, but it seems only right to keep you informed.

Your servant,
Charles Kentworthy

From Geraldine Hartford
  Shulfield Hall, Tutting-on-Cress
To Mr. Charles Kentworthy, Esq. ℅ Gavin Hartford
  8 Half Moon Street, London

21 December 1815

Mr. Kentworthy,

Thank you for telling me. I believe I have discovered the source of our troubles and I'm afraid this may all be my fault. When I sent the spell to Gavin, I informed him to buy treated dragon's breath but it appears he did not or was unable to do so. When untreated, dragon's breath is more potent as the treating process dampens the plant's magical properties. However, treating it also removes the plant's poison and makes it safe to handle. I had to wear gloves while experimenting with this spell.

Upon reading over his letter, I am increasingly convinced that Gavin has contracted Dragon Fever, an illness caused by the poison in the flower. I should have recognized this sooner when he detailed how the spell made his handkerchief catch on fire. Initially, I assumed this had happened because he had poured too much power into the spell, which he tends to do. Gavin had assumed this as well, so it did not occur to me to think beyond that. Your description of his symptoms made me reconsider that diagnosis.

I am sending with this letter a book Gavin purchased for me some time ago. You will find a recipe and an accompanying spell have been marked. It is an antidote to Dragon Fever. The local spellmaster has told me the antidote is particularly nasty, so you might have trouble getting my brother to drink it. He advised adding honey and sandalwood to the mixture as the sandalwood makes it more effective and the honey makes it slightly less repulsive.

My mother informed me she was leaving for London immediately upon reading my letter. So I imagine she will arrive within a day or so of you receiving this.

If the antidote is ineffective or if you need any more assistance, please tell me at once and I shall leave immediately.

Sincerely,
Geraldine Hartford

FROM GAVIN HARTFORD
8 Half Moon Street, London
TO GERALDINE HARTFORD
Shulfield Hall, Tutting-on-Cress

24 December 1815

DEAR GERRY,

The fever has passed but Kentworthy is still insisting on writing my letters for me, as you can probably already tell. He says you claim responsibility for my illness, but I insist you do no such thing. I completely forgot to ask the spellmaster whether or not the dragon's breath was treated. And it did not occur to me to wear gloves. Stupid of me, I now realize.

I suppose I am grateful to you for setting Mother on me. She arrived two days ago, completely certain I was on death's door. I should like to know what you told her to give her such cause for alarm. Kentworthy is giving me a stern look now and I think he thinks I am being unjust.

Oh, and Mother brought me my warming scarf. Isn't it funny how we were just talking about it? It has been very comfortable to wear. I do not know if you put the idea in her head to bring it or if she brought it of her own volition, but either way, I am glad to have it with me again. Although Kentworthy and Mother will keep fussing at it to make sure it is tucked nicely.

Happy Christmas,
Gavin

DEAR MISS HARTFORD,

Thank you for sending the instructions and the book. I enlisted the help of my friend to make the antidote. I did not trust myself to do it properly and he is one of the foremost magical talents in the country.

The antidote took effect within hours. Your brother's fever finally broke and he has been steadily improving ever since. I am continuing to ply him with the antidote, which he does not like, but he cannot fight the doctor and your mother and myself all at once, so he has had little choice.

Thank you very much for sending word to your mother. Your brother will not admit it, but I think he is glad to see her. His mouth always twitches slightly when he is pleased but trying not to show it. If he were less weary, I believe we would even be earning some of his rare smiles too.

I wish you a Happy Christmas and felicitations on the birth of your nephew.

Your servant,
Charles Kentworthy

FROM GERALDINE HARTFORD
Shulfield Hall, Tutting-on-Cress
TO GAVIN HARTFORD
8 Half Moon Street, London

27 December 1815

DEAR GAVIN,

Thank heavens you are better. I cannot forgive myself for not recognizing your symptoms sooner. Stupid of me. I am immeasurably grateful Mr. Kentworthy added his own messages to your letters. I do not think I would have realized what had caused your illness if he had not kept me informed. You know I would have been out the door in a trice if I had only received what you saw fit to tell me.

I will keep this letter brief as I do not know if you are well enough yet to respond to anything longer, and I do not wish to tire you unnecessarily. As Mr. Kentworthy pointed out in a letter to me, you tend to pour a great deal of energy into the task of letter-writing. I am certainly not complaining for I enjoy your letters immensely. But I urge you not to reply to me until you are truly well enough to do so.

Please give my regards to Mr. Kentworthy and thank him on my behalf for taking such good care of you.

Affectionately,
Gerry

From Gavin Hartford
8 Half Moon Street, London
To Geraldine Hartford
Shulfield Hall, Tutting-on-Cress

29 December 1815

Gerry,

I am better now. As you can see, I am back to writing my own letters. And I am no longer watched incessantly. Apparently, Mother and Kentworthy have finally deemed me well enough to no longer need constant observation.

We had a jolly time of it, all things considered. I rather wish you had been here. Mother came and took over in that way of hers. Thankfully, Kentworthy did not seem to mind. I do not know what you said to her, but she took a liking to him instantly. She addressed him as "the nice young man my Geraldine says has been taking care of poor Gavin." I suppose she saw him as a sort of angel of healing or some such rot. I can't say I mind, exactly, for the two of them got on famously. Unfortunately, this meant they were both coddling me incessantly and it nearly drove me to distraction.

Mother had Cook prepare a lovely dinner for Christmas Day, and Kentworthy went out and purchased gifts for both of us. Then we had our own little celebration here in the townhouse. I was worried that Mother should have left so soon after the baby was born. When I said as much, she tutted and asked why she shouldn't worry about her own child. So I suppose that was all right.

Is it not strange that I avoided asking Kentworthy about his Christmas plans out of fear of being an imposition? And not only did he spend Christmas Day with me but he has been here nearly every day for the past month.

There were a few conversations that happened before Mother arrived that I have been struggling to process on my own. I should like to tell you of them, partly to write them down and get them a little out of my own head, and partly because I should like you to help me understand them. How is it that I have come to depend on you for advice so much since I came to London?

I felt horribly guilty for having caused such a fuss the night of the casting and for never managing to give him that damned fob. And, of course, I still felt perfectly ghastly. So I was not in a very fine mood to receive him when he called on me the next day. He came in the late morning, and I had dragged myself out of bed again in an attempt to be presentable. But I was still so tired, I acted downright churlish to the poor man. He did not take offense at my attitude, but he did not look pleased either.

I learned what his look of displeasure meant when he left and came back within the hour, this time with a doctor. Between the two of them, they practically forced me to return to bed. Gerry, I was completely mortified. Imagine having your friend call a doctor on you. His own doctor, if you please. God's teeth, it was dreadful. After that, he was here every day. I slept through a great deal of it, but he seemed to always be around. And if he wasn't, the doctor was.

The first letter Kentworthy wrote to you I tried to write on my own, but he well near wrestled the pen from me. I had only gotten your name down when he took the paper, the pen, and the lap desk, and sat in a chair by my bed.

"You start your letters simply with 'Gerry?'" he said. "You do not address her as 'dear?' Is she not your closest relation?"

"I'm not you," I replied. I know this was unkind of me, but I can only say I was feeling positively wretched that day. All I could think of was you leaving Tutting-on-Cress and travelling alone to London and what Mother would say to such a thing. I couldn't sleep for thinking of it. Kentworthy finally agreed you ought to be advised as to my condition, but I did not anticipate him taking such an active hand in the matter.

At any rate, he did not quarrel with my temper. He simply said, "Have I your leave to add 'dear' to the front? It seems appropriate. The poor thing must be worried sick."

"Adding it will only make her more worried, as I never do," I said. "But, by all means, do as you wish. Shall I dictate then?"

He jotted the word down and sat, pen poised, looking at me.

I dictated the letter and after I had concluded, I saw he was still writing.

"Here, here," I said, smacking at the coverlet. "What's all this? I thought you said you weren't corresponding with my sister."

He sighed. "It would hardly constitute a correspondence, darling. If she reads your letter, she will most certainly make her way here."

"But I assured her I was fine."

"She needs someone other than yourself to tell her this, I think. If she knows you as well as I do—and she assuredly knows you better—she will believe you to be dressing up the truth."

"I never!"

He tilted his head and looked at me. I thought back to our recent dinner at which I had attempted to pretend I was in perfect health. I sighed and did not argue further.

He returned to his letter. When he was finished, he folded up the paper. Then, reaching for one of your letters on my side table, he said, "May I?"

"Don't!" I said, lunging to the side and grabbing his wrist.

It was far more energy than I had managed to expend in days and I'm sure my grip was extraordinarily weak. He did not attempt to break off my grasp, although I'm sure he could have done it easily. He only looked at my fingers, clasped around his wrist, and then turned his gaze to me, his expression steady and unreadable.

"I only wish to copy her direction," he said softly.

I felt my face flush and let go of his wrist, falling back against my pillows. "Of course," I said. "Forgive me."

He did not say anything as he wrote down your direction. I looked up when he tossed your letter back on the side table. I was relieved to see he had an amused smile on his face.

"Just what was in that letter, my dear, that you should guard it so frightfully against me?"

Quite honestly, I don't even know which letter he picked up but, hang it all, Gerry, I couldn't have the man learning how much we talk about him. It was a moment before I dared say anything. "Family business," I said at last.

He leaned back in his chair and tapped the letter he had just written against his thumbnail. "Indeed? Has John's child been born, perhaps? Sebastian undertook another escapade at Oxford? Gerry detailing her newest spell?"

I didn't reply. Of course I had told him nearly all of our family business, as he well knew.

"Is it possible you do not trust me, Gavin?" he said at last.

I looked up at that. "Nonsense," I said. "I've let you drag me all over town. That's as great a trust as I can give anyone."

"You do not trust me with your heart, I think," he said, standing up. "I will see to it this letter goes out today. You had better rest now."

I slept fitfully after that. I realized I still had not given him the watch and fob and had not managed to tell him how much I appreciated his friendship. Now he was taking care of me and I was responding to his kindness with churlishness. I'm sure he thought me quite horrid. I know I did.

The next conversation happened when I had fallen into a fever again. The doctor had prescribed laudanum and Kentworthy practically forced me to take it. So my brain was particularly foggy and I was inclined to fall asleep with little warning.

I woke up at one point to see Kentworthy sitting in a chair beside my bed, reading a book. I felt the strangest ache at seeing him keeping vigil over me and I said, before I could think better of it, "Am I a terrible friend to you, Charles?"

He was startled, for he was not aware I was awake. It was also, I think, the first time I had ever addressed him by his first name. But he revealed no surprise at my informality. He set his book aside without marking his place and leaned his arm on the bed. "Why should you think that, my dear?"

"I am so...so..." I floundered a bit and looked at him as if he could supply the right word.

He waited patiently.

"Stubborn," I finally managed.

He smiled and brushed some hair away from my forehead. "Indeed, you are, darling."

I frowned at him, feeling muddled. "And churlish."

"I have never said it," he said, letting his hand fall to my arm.

"I do not thank you properly."

"For what, dear?"

I felt something rubbing against my upper arm and looked down hazily to see his thumb stroking my sleeve.

"I do love our rides in the park," I said, looking back up at him.

He gave me a beautiful wide smile.

"Gerry says I ought to tell you. I wish she wasn't right all the time."

"I'm glad you did," he said softly.

I closed my eyes. "I have something I must give you."

"Indeed?" His thumb continued to stroke my arm.

I got the sense he was humoring me and I wanted to impress upon him that I was speaking in earnest, but I could not force my eyes back open. I fell asleep before I could say anything else.

I should like to note, Gerry, that laudanum is beastly stuff and I hope never to take it again. I had another conversation, also under its influence, that has been racketing around in my brain.

Kentworthy arrived as I was attempting to convince the doctor I did not need anymore medicine. Kentworthy looked at me with concern, and I felt embarrassed to realize he had been looking at me like that for at least a fortnight. Ashamed, I gave up my fight and surrendered to the doctor's ministrations. The doctor left and Kentworthy took up his usual seat next to the bed.

"Your sister's reply just arrived," he said, waving it in front of me. "Shall I read it to you?"

"For God's sake," I said. "I can jolly well read, Kentworthy." But my arms were feeling heavy—actually, everything felt heavy. "Oh, go on, then," I said to him.

He gave me a rueful smile and read your letter out loud. I do wish you had not gone so far as to address my concerns in your letter, however briefly. You must have known he might read it, particularly as you included a message to him. But I confess I did not expect to be laid up for so long a time, so I suppose I cannot blame you.

Kentworthy did not comment on any of it until after he had finished. Although, he did have a hard time keeping himself from laughing aloud when you called me a ninnyhammer.

"I think I like your sister a great deal," he said, folding the letters up. He set mine on my side table and tucked his into his breast pocket.

"That," I said, "does not surprise me in the least. But I do not think you should court her. I'm sure my mother would not appreciate it."

"Oh no?" he said. "Why not? I am eligible. And quite wealthy, you know."

I hope you will not be offended when I say this, but his reply made me feel strangely hollow. I was worried he might notice my distress, so I gave in to a yawn, thankful it could cover my reaction. "Yes," I said. "But you have the most colorful reputation."

He leaned back in his chair. "Anything of note?"

I thought back to your questions when I first told you I had struck up an acquaintance with him. "I think you're something of a rake."

"Perhaps," he replied. "But I flatter myself—I have not broken any hearts. I do not think most rakes can boast that."

"And you have no plans to ever marry."

"That is decidedly not true. I simply have no plans to marry for convenience. When I find someone dear enough to me, I will most certainly make a declaration. Has that rumor concerned you, darling? How sweet."

"Is it true you enjoy the company of both men and women?" You must know I was truly medicated to have had the gall to ask him that.

"I suppose you mean intimately rather than socially?"

I frowned at him, confused.

He grinned. "Let us say I find both to be lovely. Does that answer your question?"

I nodded.

"Good," he said. "Now, where on earth did you happen to hear that? I did not realize it was so generally known."

You will be angry with me, Gerry, and I cannot blame you,

but please believe me when I say it was entirely due to the laudanum that I answered, "Gerry asked me."

He gave a huff of laughter. "Good God, where does she get her information?"

I shook my head. "I wish I knew."

"What else would you like to know, my dear?"

I blinked at him.

"What else would your mother find unsuitable?"

"My mother would not be opposed to your persuasion. I did not mean to suggest—"

He laughed. "Not to worry, darling. I know better than to take what you say amiss when you're in this state. Any other concerns your mother might have?"

"Gerry said something about parties."

He chuckled and tugged the counterpane over my chest. "Those were pure fiction, I'm afraid. Lady Partridge made a joke one evening and the rumors took off. Anything else?"

I tried to think of all the things you had asked me at the start of my friendship with him. But my thoughts were muddying by this point. I shook my head.

"Good," he said. "Then I have a question of my own, before you fall back asleep."

I shifted under the covers, trying to rouse myself for what he would say next.

"What was your sister referring to when she said you ought to be kinder in your own estimation?"

This was not a question I felt comfortable answering. It was all very well for me to worry about such things to you, but to bring it up to Kentworthy himself meant I risked him discovering my many flaws before I had a chance to cure myself of them. Now that I am not under the influence of laudanum, I realize my sudden panic at this question was absurd, considering I had talked to him about it before. At the time, however, my wits were not particularly sharp. I flopped my arms on top of the counterpane and then realized his hand was still resting on it. When my hand fell on his, however, I noticed he did not pull it back.

"It is nothing."

"No," he said. "I would like to know."

My eyes started to leak a little, you know, from all of the congestion. I rubbed at them, exasperated. "It is nothing, Charles," I said.

He took one of my hands in his. "Gavin," he said. "Please tell me."

"I already told you," I said. "At least I think I did. I suppose I might have dreamt it."

"Told me what?"

"I'm a terrible friend to you."

"Ah yes. I do recall that. How long has this particular thought been fretting you?" His thumb was doing that rubbing thing again, this time over my hand.

I looked down and stared at it, a little mesmerized. "Since the fob."

"What?"

I remembered he didn't have it yet. I might have given it to him then except I couldn't get out of bed at that point. I looked back up at him. "I mean," I said. "Since the rainstorm."

"You poor, sweet man," he said. "Have you been worrying yourself this whole time?"

"I don't deserve you," I said.

His hand stilled.

"I don't deserve your friendship," I amended hastily. "You are too good to me, Charles. Have you not noticed how few friends I have? My family sent me away, for heaven's sake. It's a wonder Gerry puts up with me. I'm not at all a likeable person. Mr. Bowles was right. I'm sure I'm far too grave for you. I don't—"

"Hush," he said softly. "I did not realize it would agitate you so. We'll discuss it again later. I don't want to bring on your fever again. Forgive me, I should not have brought it up."

"Gerry brought it up," I mumbled.

"She's right, you know," he said.

"She usually is."

"You ought to be kinder to yourself."

I tried to think of a reply to this, but I was already falling back asleep.

Shortly after this, my condition worsened and all such conversations ceased. Everything was a bit of a haze for I believe I slept quite a bit. Those conversations went 'round and 'round in my head and I kept wishing I could write to you about it. Of course I'm heartily ashamed of myself now that I have finally written all of this down. I'm sure it is all tripe or laudanum-laced delirium.

But honestly, Gerry, I have not been able to stop thinking about it. I think I shall go mad. What am I to do? I had bought that gift to try to even the score between us, but now I find myself more indebted to him than ever. I had so many opportunities to give it to him too. For heaven's sake, I could have given it to him at Christmas, only I couldn't remember where I had stashed it and I did not yet have the energy to search. I can never repay him for keeping me company and seeing me to health again. Not to mention, I'm sure I made a complete cake of myself in asking him so many personal questions.

He hasn't been around at all today. Mother says it is to give her time alone with me before she leaves tomorrow. I daresay he'll be well shot of me if he were to never come back. Though I would like to give him the watch and fob. Should I get him something more now?

Affectionately,

Gavin

P.S. This letter should be accompanying a package of gifts. There are little things for our aunt and uncle and cousins and several things for you. I would have liked to send them to you before the holiday but, well, naturally that did not happen. I also completely missed your birthday, which is a shame, because I had these presents prepared to send to you. I hope you had a happy Christmas and a happy birthday.

P.P.S. I am also sending back the book. I'm glad it came to be of such use. I'm sure neither of us could have predicted that. I still feel a right fool for forgetting all of your warnings about dragon's breath. I know I shall never make the same mistake again, not after being sick for nearly a month and certainly not after that horrid medicine.

Kentworthy was dreadfully nervous when he fed the medicine to me. I tell you, Gerry, his hand was positively trembling. I have never seen him so unnerved. Except, I suppose, when I jumped into Peerless Pond. Oh, and when I started to fall ill. Good God, how do I manage to always upset the poor man's calm? On the other hand, he did look excessively pleased when I started to feel better. It almost made taking the antidote worth it. Almost.

FROM GERALDINE HARTFORD
Shulfield Hall, Tutting-on-Cress
TO GAVIN HARTFORD
8 Half Moon Street, London

2 January 1816

DEAR GAVIN,

I am glad you are feeling well enough to write your own letters again. As I think you know, the baby was born while you were ill. I do not know what Mama told you on the subject. From what she has told me, however, it seems Veronica has taken to motherhood in her usual stride—which is to say, she complains about everything and is never satisfied. I think Mama had hoped this would end when the baby was born, but I never had such expectations. I believe Papa keeps to his study and John has taken to being out of the house as much as possible.

Thank you kindly for your gifts. Everyone here has asked me to send their thanks as well. I greatly appreciated the sweet little notebook you sent. I have already begun to use it for planning out my experiments. I am sending your gifts as well. Uncle Gregory embroidered the handkerchiefs. After he gave them to me to send on to you, I put a spell into each of them to increase their ability to absorb water. You can inform Mr. Kentworthy that the next time he needs to dry you or your hair, he can use one of these and they should do the job creditably. I suspect you will not tell him this, but you can be sure I will when I finally meet the gentleman. You do have a tendency to get yourself in scrapes when you are with him. If it were anyone else, I would be concerned. But you are so very solemn and careful as a rule, I really think these occasional lapses in judgment might actually be good for you, in a way.

I am glad to hear Mama liked Mr. Kentworthy. I confess, I am a little disappointed I did not get to meet him first. But it sounds as if she approved of him and that is, I find, half the battle.

The other half of the battle, Gavin, will be in you being honest with yourself. It is increasingly plain to me that you care a great deal for Mr. Kentworthy. You may not choose to admit it, of course. But it is highly unusual for you to go out of your way to purchase a very expensive gift for a friend.

From what I've read in your letters, I suspect Mr. Kentworthy might feel the same way for you. He certainly feels a great deal of affection for you, but I do not know him well enough to know if his feelings run deeper than that. I will say, however, one does not usually keep vigil at a friend's bedside for nearly a month—and at Christmastime—if one does not care deeply for the person. I would even hazard a guess that he loves you. Again, I do not know the gentleman, so I cannot say this with complete certainty. I can say I have held this suspicion for quite some time. The way you describe his behavior towards you and the way he talks to you—well, it certainly does not take much imagination. I should also add that Mama wrote of him in such praising tones, I would be very much surprised if she did not consider him to be courting you. Again, I have not had the pleasure to meet him yet, so I am going entirely off your descriptions and Mama's.

Is it not just a little bit possible that you love him in return? I do not say this to push you in one direction or another. I only want you to consider it as a possibility. You would not be happy if you were to spend the rest of your life alone, even if you would never admit it. I'd hate to see you living in isolation because you feel it is your only option.

As to your previous letter, I suspect your maudlin thoughts were due, in part, to the chill you caught from the pond and the rain. Although you have, it seems, taken those thoughts to heart, which is just like you. I could fill pages with why I enjoy your company, but I feel sure this would not satisfy you nor cure your doubts. I think it is good that you care enough for Mr. Kentworthy to have bought him a gift, but you cannot think gifts are your only proof that you are a worthy friend. You do not enjoy Mr. Kentworthy's company solely because he has gifted you with books. It has been some time since he has done so and yet your connection has only become stronger.

And I am glad to hear you admit when I am right. You ought to stop doubting us, Mr. Kentworthy and me. We know what we are about.

With love,
Gerry

FROM SEBASTIAN HARTFORD
   Digory College, Oxford
TO GAVIN HARTFORD
   8 Half Moon Street, London

3 January 1816

WHAT HO, GAVIN!

Are you still alive? Father said you were quite ill and that is why neither you nor Mama were at home for Christmas. I do hope you're all right. But I must admit it was an absolute wrench celebrating Christmas with only Father, John, and Veronica. I mean, really! There were ever so many lectures!

At one point, I couldn't take it anymore and put a spell on Veronica's hand mirror so it didn't reflect her face. Such a laugh! She was positively steaming. Oddly enough, Father did not say anything about it, but John read me a fine sermon on how I need to grow up. So then I put a spell on all of his shoes to make them squeak every five steps. It was hilarious! He kept stopping to check them and he couldn't figure it out for days. Father did talk to me about that one. Although, frankly, I suspect it's because he had grown tired of all the squeaking.

I did get to see Mama before I went back to Oxford. She had all manner of nice things to say about your Mr. Kentworthy. I'm a trifle jealous, to be completely honest. Imagine having someone sitting at your bedside for a month while you're ill! I don't suppose anyone would do such a romantic thing for me. You get all the luck. I asked her if he was as handsome as everyone says and then Father said if I paid as much attention to my studies as I did to handsome faces, he wouldn't worry about me half so much. Which is dashed unfair! After all, I wouldn't need my studies if I found the right handsome face, would I? I declare, I would easily pick marriage over further schooling without a backwards look.

Anyway, glad you're not dead.
Affectionately,
Seb

FROM REGINALD HARTFORD
Lynnwood House, Sherton
TO GAVIN HARTFORD
8 Half Moon Street, London

4 January 1816

GAVIN,

I am relieved to know that you are out of danger. If it were not for Sebastian's return from school, I would have traveled to London as well. However, as I needed to speak to your younger brother, I entrusted your care to your mother's capable hands. She has assured me that you do not need to return to Sherton for some convalescence. From what she has described of your friend in town, you are being well looked after. I am sure I do not need to tell you, Gavin, that we are both very pleased to know you are making friends. She was quite impressed by your Mr. Kentworthy. I look forward to making his acquaintance.

Do rest before you continue your work as steward. Nothing I have tasked you with is pressing.

Father

FROM GAVIN HARTFORD
8 Half Moon Street, London
TO GERALDINE HARTFORD
Shulfield Hall, Tutting-on-Cress

5 January 1816

GERRY,

I am relieved by your response to my inanities in the previous letter. I do not know if you are correct in your assessment of the situation. However, since you so often are, I will consider, as you requested. I own Kentworthy must feel some affection towards me, as a friend, but I do not believe it to run any deeper than friendship. It has occurred to me he may only feel pity for me. It would explain everything he has done so far, including his kindness when I was ill.

As for the rest, I am not sure of my own feelings on the matter. That is to say, I *am* sure of my feelings, but I am dreadfully fearful of exploring them, only to have them disappointed. You will deny it, of course, but you are overly generous with me. You always have been. It is possible that I am overly critical of myself, but I already struggle believing myself worthy of Kentworthy's friendship. How could I possibly ever be worthy of more? It does not bear thinking, Gerry. I daresay I have much to be thankful for already. What could it possibly serve to wish for what I could never have? Please do not press me on the subject.

Kentworthy took me to Vauxhall Gardens the other night to celebrate the New Year and we watched the fireworks display. I drank one glass of arrack-punch before he refilled my cup with water. I fear he no longer trusts me with alcohol. Do you see what I mean? Pity truly seems to be driving a great deal of his actions.

We ran into Viscount Finlington while we were there and I am pleased to report that, for once, I did not act like an utter fool in front of the gentleman. I asked him how he learned to master Motion spells so easily and he laughed, chucked me under the chin, and said my skills of observation were "scrumptious." He did not answer my question. Kentworthy explained to him that my sister is a proficient spellcaster and has been learning spell-building. I was worried he would go into details about my foolishness with the dragon's breath but, thankfully, he was circumspect on that point.

Finlington did ask a great deal about you, though. After hearing all about you, Finlington asked me about my own talents. Kentworthy was shockingly eloquent on the subject as well. In the end, Finlington requested to be present sometime when I cast one of your spells and he declared himself desirous to meet you. In fact, he learned more about both of our talents in magic than I learned about his.

It occurs to me that the viscount is a very private person, for all his outrageousness and eccentricities. I mentioned this to Kentworthy later and commented that the gentleman's reluctance to speak about himself made me all the more curious about him. Kentworthy laughed and said, "Now you know how it feels, darling." Which, of course, makes no sense whatsoever.

Affectionately,

Gavin

P.S. We are to attend a ball in a few days and I am living in dread of it. I have not had occasion to go to a ball, which is no mean feat when I have been in London for so many months. I suppose I ought to count myself lucky.

FROM GERALDINE HARTFORD
Shulfield Hall, Tutting-on-Cress
TO GAVIN HARTFORD
8 Half Moon Street, London

8 January 1816

DEAR GAVIN,

Your description of Vauxhall was shabby to the extreme. You must tell me what you thought of it.

I confess I am a little shocked to learn that Viscount Finlington was asking about me. Please tell me you did not tell him anything embarrassing. Better yet, ask Mr. Kentworthy if you said anything embarrassing, for you know I do not trust your judgment on the subject.

I have many thoughts regarding the sentiments expressed in your previous letter. You asked me not to press you and so I shall not, except to say this: if you trust Mr. Kentworthy as much as you claim, why do you not trust his judgment where you are concerned?

Please tell me absolutely everything about the ball. I wish to know who hosted it, who you danced with, and anyone you recognized in attendance. I do not know when you are going, but I am sending a spell packet for you should you receive it in time. It is a spell to prolong the comfort of a pair of shoes. It is one of Mr. Fenshaw's designs. I believe it is used around here by the laborers who are on their feet all day, but Julia recommended it to me once for dancing, so I thought you might appreciate it for your upcoming event.

Affectionately,
Gerry

FROM GAVIN HARTFORD
8 Half Moon Street, London
TO SEBASTIAN HARTFORD
Digory College, Oxford

9 January 1816

SEB,

No, I am not dead. Yes, I am all right. Thank you for your concerns, I think. I honestly cannot tell if you expressed any.

I am sure that was not a very enjoyable Christmas for you. I am sorry I could not be there. Although, you really are a pinhead to actually play pranks right in front of Father. Not saying John and Veronica didn't deserve it. But, really, Seb. It was hardly your smartest decision.

I disagree with your assessment on your studies being less important than a prospective match, but your comment has given me some cause for speculation. Is your constant request to be sent for indicative of an unhappiness in being at Oxford? I hope you will tell me if that is the case. You know none of us would want you to be unhappy. I'm sure Father would arrange a tutor for you or something if you really hated it.

Affectionately,
Gavin

FROM GAVIN HARTFORD
8 Half Moon Street, London
TO GERALDINE HARTFORD
Shulfield Hall, Tutting-on-Cress

11 January 1816

GERRY,

We went to the ball last night. Your letter arrived yesterday afternoon so I was able to place the spell on my shoes beforehand. It worked a treat. Thank you very much for sending it.

Kentworthy came to pick me up, although he arrived earlier than expected and came inside the house to make sure I was dressed to his exacting standards. I am pleased to tell you he was very satisfied with my cravat. I tried a more difficult one for the occasion. I do believe I've come a long way in that regard and I cannot believe this is something I care to be proud of. But there it is.

He gave a small tweak to the knot and said, "You look a picture, darling. I daresay there will be many ladies and gentlemen who hope to secure a dance with you. I shall be hard pressed to see you don't overexert yourself tonight."

This comment put me in a dreadfully nervous state. The fact is, Gerry, you are the only person who has any idea where my preferences lie. I know I have never admitted it outright but given recent topics discussed, I have no doubt you are aware of my feelings. Although, now that I think on it, Mr. Bowles said he had a good guess, which I assume to be correct, looking back on the conversation.

At any rate, I have been so diligent about keeping this aspect of my character a secret, I have never danced with a gentleman before—other than our brothers, and that certainly does not count, for that was merely fulfilling an obligation (and because Seb is such an absurd enthusiast for the pastime). The realization that I would likely dance with another gentleman for the first time, in public, at a London ball, had me completely terrified.

I'm sure I learned the steps for following—I am a second-born, after all—you know how it is at Sherton. Mr. Collinger was dead-set against the waltz, so it was hardly ever played. Even when it was, I have rarely been inclined to dance. I only ever stood up with you or Seb to help make up the couples.

There is certainly no issue in knowing how to lead, but that is usually the position taken by the one initiating the dance—you know, firstborns or people with large fortunes. I would never ask someone to dance with me, so I really ought to have been a better pupil in terms of dance lessons.

You and Seb know the follower's side since you both showed your inclinations at an early age. I have always been certain if I were to stand up with a gentleman, you, Mother, John, and Seb would all pounce upon the proof. Standing up with a lady would give everyone the wrong impression. It always seemed simpler to just abstain from dancing as much as possible. I did not know how to confess all of this to Kentworthy, so I sat in agony for half of the ride, trying to determine how to broach the subject.

In the end, I didn't have to because he noticed. "Are you all right, my dear?" he said. "You seem very tense."

I suppose I could have put him off with a comment about being nervous in attending the ball. While that was certainly true, it didn't feel right; I owe him so much, my honesty being the least of the things he deserves from me. So I said, "I have been thinking about what you said before we left. About ladies and gentlemen wishing to dance with me."

It was dark in the carriage so I could not see his face. But his voice was soft when he said, "Does that upset you?"

"Well," I said. "The fact is…I've never danced with another gentleman before. I learned how to follow, but I'm sure I don't remember. I should hate to make a cake of myself."

"Ah," he said. "Well, that is no great hardship, darling. You can simply avoid the waltz and other such dances. We can see to it your card is only filled with cotillions and quadrilles. The steps for those are very much the same, regardless of the side of the line you are on." He paused. "Do I take it, then, that you would not be opposed to dancing with another man?"

"I..." I hesitated.

"Forgive me for asking. You do not have to tell me," he said. "Unless you wish to. I know you are private about such things."

"No, I wish to tell you." I took a deep breath. "The fact is, my family is dreadfully nosy. I've always been private about it because I know I should be forced to withstand a parade of possible suitors otherwise. And that is...undesirable."

"Why undesirable?"

I sighed. "I have no talent for talking to people." I glanced at him briefly and then looked away. "Particularly people who I happen to find attractive. No one else in my family struggles with this. John always feels as if he is the cleverest person in the room. Gerry makes a million friends wherever she goes. And Seb, well, he lacks all subtlety, but I don't believe he's ever had a problem forming new acquaintances. At any rate, none of my family would understand. I have no desire to look a fool. Although I daresay I do that often enough with you."

He leaned forward so his face was occasionally illuminated by the passing streetlamps. "Gavin," he said, his voice gentle. "I have introduced you to any number of people in the past few months. You do not give yourself enough credit, darling. Everyone adores you."

I gave him a dubious look.

"It is no secret you are a young man of reserved temperament. No one minds it, I assure you. Besides," he added, with a small smile. "I rather think it adds quite uniquely to your charms."

"It is very kind of you to say so. And in answer to your question," I pressed on, before he could comment. "You are correct. I am not opposed to dancing with other men."

There was silence in the carriage for a moment, long enough for me to wish I hadn't said anything.

At last, he said, "Thank you, darling. I am honored by

your confidence." He sat back in his seat. "Will you be accepting offers to dance, then?"

I took a shaky breath. "I suppose so. I daresay it's foolish, but I'm a trifle daunted by the prospect."

He chuckled. "Not foolish at all, dear. Would it help if your first dance was with a friend? I would be delighted to dance with you."

I scarcely dared to breathe, his offer affected me that much. Finally, I said, "Thank you. I believe it would."

We arrived at the ball shortly after. It was hosted by Lord and Lady Kensley. A very fine affair. The lemonade was kept deliciously cool and the room was not as stuffy as I had expected. I must commend the hosts for keeping such good spellcasters on staff. It is hard to keep drinks cool and a room full of people comfortable. They must have hired a whole troop of talented spellcasters.

Kentworthy made a point of doing a round through each of the rooms to see who was in attendance. I recognized a few people I have met over the course of my time in London: Lady and Lord Partridge, Viscount Finlington, Miss Cartwright, and some people I know from my rides in Hyde Park. I was still dreadfully nervous, but it was nice to see familiar faces. It made me feel as though I was on more solid ground.

Kentworthy completed our circuit in the ballroom and then walked me to where the dance cards were being handed out. We stood to the side to watch the dancers complete the set. He took the pencil and carefully drew a line through all of the dances entailing leaders and followers. Then, just as carefully, he wrote his name in the first open line before handing the card back to me. He showed me how to slip it on my wrist to indicate my station as a younger sibling and my status as available for dances.

He pointed out some of the differences with the people dancing as followers. "Do you see how he's bowing there while the ladies are curtsying?" or "Notice how he is going under his partner's arm" or "Look there, she puts her hand on top of her partner's, rather like she is alighting from a carriage." He said all of this in a low voice so I might be the only one to hear it. It was dashed kind of him. Despite my embarrassment, I confess I was grateful for the information.

When the set ended, he turned to me and said, "Shall we?"

I did not feel prepared for it, but I nodded anyway and allowed him to lead me onto the floor. It felt daring stepping onto the floor with another gentleman, and with Kentworthy of all people. He is so frightfully popular. I will have to admit that as uncomfortable as I felt, it did seem uniquely right, for once, to take a partner in a dance; it has always been a sort of social obligation, something expected of me. As such, I have never really appreciated the appeal of dancing. But joining someone who I actually like and respect, well, it felt intimate. I was very flustered by the experience, I need hardly tell you. But I enjoyed it too.

Viscount Finlington found us after the set. "You are a superb dancer, darling," he told me. "You two look very fine together. Such an attractive couple you make."

The music started up for the next set and I took a drink off a passing tray so they wouldn't see how much I was blushing.

"Will you do me the honor of the next dance, m'dear?" the viscount asked.

I glanced at Kentworthy, who was looking at me in that amused way of his. I stammered that I would be delighted.

"Splendid!" Finlington said. He held his hand out and I passed him my dance card. He very politely did not comment on the dances Kentworthy had crossed off and he wrote his name for the next dance. When he passed the card back to me, I fumbled a bit in remembering which wrist to put it on. I fumbled even more when I tried to put it on without spilling the drink in my hand.

"You sweet thing," Finlington said as he took the card back and helped me slip it on. "Don't tell me this is your first ball in London?"

I nodded.

"Really, Charlie," he said. "I'm surprised at you. You took this darling man to Covent Garden before taking him to a ball? You are an abominable guide, m'dear."

"That was certainly a miscalculation on my part. But, to my credit, I did not intend for us to actually interact with anyone."

I was a little startled to realize the viscount knew of our Covent Garden adventure. I wondered, suddenly, what else the man knew. I took another sip of my drink in an attempt to mask my shock at this revelation.

"I suppose even you are due for a misstep occasionally, my sweet," Finlington said. "But do you really mean to tell me you've known dear Mr. Hartford for months and you're only just now bringing him to a ball?"

Kentworthy smiled and took two drinks off a tray, passing one to Finlington. "One must learn to crawl before attempting to walk, Bertie," he said.

Finlington threw back his head and laughed. When the next set started, he led me onto the floor. I'm sure it was my imagination, but I could feel people staring at me. I suppose it's not to be wondered at, considering the fact that I stood up with both Kentworthy and Finlington. After the dance, Finlington offered his arm as we stepped off the dance floor, and I realized Kentworthy was not where we left him. I began to look around the room, trying to find him.

"Oh, don't worry, darling," the viscount said, patting my hand. "He was summoned into another room while we were dancing."

"Summoned? By who?"

"The Dukex of Molbury."

"Oh," I said. "I didn't realize they were in attendance. I've heard about them a good deal since I arrived. Aren't they very important?"

"I would certainly say so. And they just got back from France, so you'll likely see them at a great many places now."

"I doubt that, my lord," I said. "I'm not so grand as to be in the dukex's circle."

"Oh no?" he replied with a grin.

I felt a small curl of dread in my stomach. "Don't tell me you know them."

"Even better, darling. We're cousins. And I'm going to introduce you." So saying, he clapped his hand over mine as if to keep me from running away and led me into the next room. "Don't fret," he said, giving my hand a squeeze. "If they've been talking to Charlie this whole time, they're likely dying to meet you by now. My cousin can be a frightful dragon of a person, but I have no doubt they'll like you."

This did not make me feel any better, but I couldn't very well protest. The viscount led me to a corner of the room where Kentworthy was perched on a little settee next to an older person.

You know as well as I do that our village is too small to provide varied company. So even though I am fully aware there are people who discover they fall outside the lines of the gender they've been taught to believe, and there are people who are neither men nor women, and there are people who fluctuate between genders, I've never met anyone from any of those categories. I will say this for London, it certainly offers a person a far more varied society.

The dukex turned out to be a short and round individual with regal bearing. I would guess them to be in their fifties, at least. Possibly even in their sixties, although they had a handsome face that made it difficult to determine age. They wore an elegant suit and a perfectly tied cravat but had a silver band in their hair with a plume of feathers attached to it. Everything in their outfit was well coordinated and exceedingly elegant, from their ruby cravat pin to the scarlet feathers in their hair and the fan they held to match. They noticed us first and tapped Kentworthy with the fan to alert him.

Kentworthy stood to greet us and Viscount Finlington made the introductions. "Your Grace," he said. "Allow me to introduce Mr. Gavin Hartford. Mr. Hartford, this is the Dukex of Molbury."

I bowed, feeling awkward to have such august attention on me. I felt even more awkward when the dukex looked me up and down in a critical way. I could see some familial resemblance between the viscount and his cousin. They had similar complexions and hair color, and the dukex had a full mouth that tipped up at the corners, similar to the viscount. But their eyes were a bright blue instead of grey and their cheeks were lightly rouged.

They held out a languid hand to me, and I bent over it and kissed their knuckles. Then they said, "Do sit down, Mr. Hartford."

I nervously took the seat Kentworthy had vacated. The dukex turned back to Kentworthy and said, "Be a dear and fetch me a glass of lemonade, won't you? I'm quite parched. I fancy the table in the blue room had stronger cooling spells. Be so good as to go there."

Kentworthy looked as if he very much wanted to object, but he glanced at Finlington before turning back to the dukex and said, "But of course, Your Grace."

The dukex leaned against the cushions and gave me another once-over. "Well, I can certainly see what the fuss was all about."

I had no idea what to say to that. I folded my hands in my lap.

"Tell me about yourself."

I blinked at them. "What is it you would like to know, Your Grace?"

"I take it you are not a firstborn. Let's start there."

"I'm the secondborn sibling, Your Grace. I'm from a little village called Sherton."

"Do you have any younger siblings?"

"Yes, Your Grace. I have a sister who is two years younger and a brother who is seven years younger."

"How old are you?"

"Five and twenty."

"Are your siblings as good-looking as you are?"

"Er...there is a very strong family resemblance."

"Well, that's certainly fortunate. You shall have to bring them to me when they come out into society."

"My sister is already out, Your Grace. She had her first Season last spring. She's staying with my cousins now, but I imagine she'll come back to London for the Season."

"Charles told me this is your first time in London. Do you mean to tell me your younger sister came out before you?"

"Yes, Your Grace. She's much more...social than I am. My parents were kind enough to understand that I was not yet ready."

"Well, I will most assuredly have words with your parents if ever I meet them. It doesn't do a young person a bit of good to delay coming out into society." They gave a small smile and patted my cheek. "Don't look so alarmed, child. You are certainly not to blame. And anyway, I suppose it matters little now. Do you all have a dowry?"

I was startled by the question. I glanced up at Viscount Finlington, who gave me an encouraging smile. "About five thousand pounds."

The dukex raised an eyebrow. "Well," they said. "Money isn't everything. And with such a pretty face, I can't imagine your modest fortune will be much of an issue."

I blushed and looked down. The dukex curled a finger under my chin and directed my gaze back up. "No need to blush so, child. It is a good thing to have attractive physical attributes. As a younger sibling, you will certainly want all of the help you can get in making a good match. Wealth and beauty do much to recommend a person, but there are other factors. Whereabouts in London are you situated?"

"Mayfair, Your Grace. Half Moon Street."

"Fashionable enough. Do you belong to a club?"

"We are members at Nesbit's."

"Really? Same as Charles and Bertram then. You must come from a good sort of family. That helps a great deal." They tilted my face to the side a little. "You have very nice cheekbones, my dear. When you have your portraits done, see to it the lighting in the room emphasizes this."

"Portraits, Your Grace? I'm sorry, I don't understand you."

Their mouth quirked up. "I must say I'm surprised. Charles is not known for his subtlety." To my relief, they dropped their hold on my chin. Then they tapped their fan against my clenched hands. "A bit of advice, poppet. Society is like a dangerous beast: best not to show your fear. Show respect, of course, but never fear. They can smell fear, you know. They'll devour you alive."

I swallowed, unsure of how to respond. But I took the hint and unclenched my hands and laid them on my knees.

The dukex gave me a warm smile. "I was sure Charles was exaggerating about your sweet nature. How novel that he was actually correct for once."

Kentworthy returned at that juncture. He bowed and handed a glass of lemonade to the dukex. Then he smiled at me. "Glad to see you're still in one piece, my dear. Are you done interrogating him yet?" he added to the dukex.

The dukex sipped the lemonade and then set it aside. "Far from it. I have a great many more questions."

"It is his first London ball. Can you not ask him these questions another time?"

They leveled Kentworthy with a look. "Do you want me to send you on another errand?"

Kentworthy sighed and gave a little bow in acquiescence.

The dukex turned back to me. "Who is staying in London with you?"

"I'm staying here alone, Your Grace. Although Mr. Kentworthy has seen to it I'm not spending all of my time alone," I said, feeling myself blush at the words.

Their eyes narrowed. "What, no chaperone, child?"

"I am here on business, Your Grace."

They turned back to Kentworthy. "Charles."

"We met at the club, darling. You would not tell him he is not allowed to go to his club alone, would you?"

"I most certainly would. Furthermore, I would tell him that a nextborn who has not reached their majority has no business traipsing about London with eligible firstborns unchaperoned. For his first time in town, his parents ought to be with him or at least his older sibling. Why is no one here to look after you, child?" they said, pinning me with a frown.

"My brother just had a baby," I stammered. "That is, his wife did. My mother is at home helping them since this is their firstborn. My father doesn't like town. I'm technically here to see to my father's business interests and to look after our townhouse, not really for society at all."

The dukex pursed their lips. "I shall most certainly have words with them." They sighed and patted my hand where it rested on my knee. "Well, don't worry, poppet. I shall see to it you're properly looked after."

"Is that really necessary?" Kentworthy said.

The dukex glared at him and scooped up my hand to clasp it between both of theirs. The gesture was oddly protective in nature and made me feel like the child they kept calling me.

"I might add, Your Grace," Finlington said with a small smile, "that dear Mr. Hartford is always adorably proper. I'm sure you have nothing to fear on that account."

"I am pleased to hear it. Although I'm not surprised, given what I've seen of him. But his good behavior does not exclude him from being talked of. Are you being careful with his reputation, Charles?"

Kentworthy looked almost angry at that. "Of course I am."

They gave Kentworthy a considering look. "I admit I haven't heard any gossip about you lately. So it would seem you've been shockingly well-behaved since I've been away."

Kentworthy's irritation gave way to mock affront. "You wound me, darling."

"And you, *darling*, are very lucky I've been out of the country," they retorted. "I'm sure I would have seen to it that this child had a chaperone. Not to mention a far more active social calendar. And he would most certainly not still be unattached."

"With all due respect, Your Grace, I have provided him with a very busy calendar."

"Yes, yes." The dukex waved their fan dismissively. "You told me all about the boxing lessons and the rides in the park. That's all very well and good, but this boy has been in town for how long?" They looked at me.

"Since September," I murmured.

They raised an eyebrow at Kentworthy. "Four months and one ball?" They smirked. "Really, Charles. You're slipping."

Kentworthy looked amused. "I can't say I'm disappointed you've been out of the country, darling. Much as I adore your good company. I know my friend well enough to know he would not be happy with a drawing room full of suitors, which is most certainly what would happen if you were in charge."

The dukex turned back to me and squeezed my hand. "What do you say, poppet? I could make you the most sought-after nextborn in town within a fortnight."

I felt myself pale at the words, but I did not know of an appropriate way to turn them down.

In the end, I didn't need to. They seemed to notice my

144 | SARAH WALLACE

anguish and chuckled. "My word, you are sweet." They turned back to Kentworthy. "Very well, I'll let you have your way for now. But know this," they added, pointing their fan at him. "I want to be kept abreast of the situation. I shall desire further acquaintance with him and you will accept all my invitations, or I shall know the reason. If I think you are not being careful enough, I will take over. Understood?"

Kentworthy took a deep breath. "Understood."

"And if this boy is not married by the Season's start, he's going under my wing."

I was much alarmed by this, but Kentworthy merely looked thoughtful. "Can we not settle for engaged, Your Grace?"

They scoffed. "Do you think you can manage it?"

"I certainly hope so."

They gave him a shrewd look and then studied me in much the same way. "Very well," they said at last, turning back to him. "I will allow it. But take care, Charles. For I'm apt to change my mind, you know."

"Duly noted," Kentworthy said with a bow. "Can I have my friend back now, please?"

The dukex tutted. "Very well. Off you go. A pleasure to meet you, Mr. Hartford. Bertram, sit. I should like to talk to you."

They patted my hand and then released it. I stood up hastily before they could change their mind. The viscount gave me a wink as he slid into the seat. Kentworthy put a hand to my back and guided me swiftly out of the room.

"Good God, they're so nosy," he muttered. "I am sorry, my dear. I would have warned you if I had known."

"I'm all right," I said. "I didn't know you were acquainted with them. But I suppose I shouldn't be surprised. You seem to know everybody."

He grinned. "Bertie and I have been friends for our entire lives. The dukex is a prominent member of Bertie's family.

They were something of a fixture in Bertie's life and, thus, mine as well. I don't have much of a family, you know, so the dukex was a sort of parental figure for me. I've looked up to them for years and they've always been very kind to me. I'm glad they liked you so well, for it is good to have their approval. But I confess I did not anticipate them taking such an active hand. It is dashed unsettling."

"I didn't know you don't have much of a family," I said, latching on to this bit of information.

"Didn't you?"

I shook my head. "I tell you about my family all the time, but you've never talked about yours. I always thought you were private about it or something." I felt myself blush at the statement. "Stupid of me, now that I think about it."

"Not stupid at all, darling."

"I ought to have asked you."

"I'm not complaining."

Despite his assurances, I felt rather agitated at the additional proof of how little I deserved his friendship. I think he must have noticed my agitation, for he added, "Please don't fret about it, my dear. I am truly not offended."

"I am such a terrible friend to—"

"Hush," he said gently. "Let's not say another word about it. I'll tell you anything you wish to know later. All right?"

I nodded. I would have pressed the matter further, but he walked me to where Lady and Lord Partridge were standing and our conversation was cut short. To my surprise, Lady Partridge asked for my dance card and wrote her name for the next set.

I danced far more last night than I ever have in my life. Viscount Finlington rejoined us after his interview with his cousin was concluded. It was quite nice to be surrounded by people I knew for the whole evening. And two men and one lady who I had never met before approached our party for an introduction to me before asking for a dance. Really, it was a dizzying experience. And Kentworthy claimed two more dances before the evening was over.

Kentworthy was very solicitous all evening. As he had been at Vauxhall Gardens, he was particular about making sure I did not drink very much. He saw to it I never danced two dances in a row, insisting I rested for at least one full set. I'll admit it was rather embarrassing to be coddled in such a way, but I can't deny I was relieved. I was exhausted by the end of the evening. The spell on the shoes worked very well, but I danced so much my feet are sore despite the magic. I have applied a balm to my feet, which has been helping. Thankfully, Kentworthy told me we are not going riding today and I am grateful; we were up shockingly late. I know I could have never risen in time for our usual appointment.

I hope my account of the evening is detailed enough for your satisfaction.

If you would be so kind as to send another packet of your spell, I am well enough now to cast it. I would like to give Kentworthy a better evening than what I offered him last time. It is, I think, the very least I can do after all he has done for me.

Affectionately,

Gavin

P.S. The butler just came in to say that I have callers. I have never had callers before. He handed me their card and I didn't recognize the name. I would ask your advice, but you will not be able to advise me quickly enough. I shall have to determine what to do. I've asked him to tell them I'm not available at the moment, but I very much hope it doesn't happen again.

From Gavin Hartford
8 Half Moon Street, London
To Charles Kentworthy, Esq.
16 Berkeley Square, London

11 January 1816

Kentworthy,

I hope you will not think it amiss if I ask your advice on something. I have now received three calls from complete strangers. I haven't the faintest notion of why it's happening, nor what to do about it. Under normal circumstances, I would ask my sister for advice, but she is too far away to help. Please tell me what I should do. I'm at my wits' end, I need hardly tell you.

Hartford

From Charles Kentworthy, Esq.
16 Berkeley Square, London
To Gavin Hartford
8 Half Moon Street, London

11 January 1816

Dear Gavin,

Only you would find such a thing a mysterious occurrence. You were seen out and about at a ball and people now wish to meet you. It is quite unsurprising, I assure you. However, as to what you ought to do about it, I confess I am uncertain. I shall ask the Dukex of Molbury if it would be acceptable for you to receive callers without a chaperone. They will definitely know. In the meantime, you might do well to have your butler tell people you are not at home. We can delay our usual appointment in the park until we have rectified this situation.

Charles

FROM GAVIN HARTFORD
8 Half Moon Street, London
TO CHARLES KENTWORTHY, ESQ.
16 Berkeley Square, London

11 January 1816

KENTWORTHY,

I am indeed grateful for that advice. I have told my butler I am currently not at home to callers, as you suggested, but I did give him your name as an exception.

Hartford

FROM CHARLES KENTWORTHY, ESQ.
16 Berkeley Square, London
TO GAVIN HARTFORD
8 Half Moon Street, London

11 January 1816

GAVIN,

The dukex's exact words were: "under no account should he accept callers without a chaperone." Their advice was that you continue to be unavailable to anyone you have not already met. You might do well to give your butler a list of your acquaintances.

Perhaps we should meet at the club for dinner tonight.

Charles

• • •

FROM GAVIN HARTFORD
8 Half Moon Street, London
TO CHARLES KENTWORTHY, ESQ.
16 Berkeley Square, London

11 January 1816

KENTWORTHY,

I cannot thank you enough. Please pass on my thanks to the dukex as well. I have followed your and their advice and given a list to the butler of my acquaintances.

I shall meet you in the club at the usual time.
Hartford

FROM GERALDINE HARTFORD
Shulfield Hall, Tutting-on-Cress
TO GAVIN HARTFORD
8 Half Moon Street, London

13 January 1816

DEAR GAVIN,

My word, that evening sounds marvelous! I know you asked me not to press you, but really. Three dances? You do realize that generally means something, don't you?

I cannot believe you met the Dukex of Molbury. It is hilarious, really, that out of everyone in our family, you have made the most impressive social connections. I wonder if I shall meet them when I return to London. Do you think they might get us vouchers for Almacks? I am not suggesting you ask them, of course. But all the same, I am quite thrilled at the prospect of meeting such a grand person.

Who were the people who asked to dance with you? Is Mr. Kentworthy a good dancer? And Viscount Finlington?

Honestly, even when you do provide details in your letters, you leave so many interesting things out.

I have some news from Tutting-on-Cress, incidentally. Rose and Julia are to be married. They have set the date two months hence so they may have everything prepared. Aunt Lily is in raptures. Please say you will come. And if you were to bring Mr. Kentworthy with you, I would like it above all things. I'm sure you will object to the notion with fears of being an imposition, but as someone who has attended many balls in my London Season, I can only say: three dances with the same person is a very particular mark of interest. Mama would not have permitted me three dances with anybody.

I hope you are not still fretting about knowing so little about Mr. Kentworthy's family. From what you've described of him, he does not seem at all shy, but he may still be private about some things. He did not seem bothered by your ignorance, in any case.

I probably ought to have warned you that we always had callers after attending a formal event. They are likely people who want to meet you. I think it is quite normal, but I am not sure if you can meet new people without a chaperone. Perhaps you could write to the Dukex of Molbury about it? I feel sure they could advise you, and they did seem to like you.

Please find the enclosed spell. I hope your casting is more successful this time. I was also able to scrounge up some treated dragon's breath.

Affectionately,
Gerry

FROM JOHN HARTFORD
Lynnwood House, Sherton
TO GAVIN HARTFORD
8 Half Moon Street, London

14 January 1816

GAV,

Once again, you failed to respond to my letters. I have given the matter a great deal of thought. I must conclude that your lack of responses to my numerous offers for help are rooted in the fact that I was correct all along. You were sent to London without any proper preparation. Thus you are at sea. I wish you could have said as much in a letter, but I suppose I ought to take some share of the blame. After all, I am your older brother. I have known you all your life and I am well versed in your tiresome moods.

The infant was born. I might add we never received a congratulatory letter from you, not even after you recovered from your illness. You really do have the most appalling manners. Veronica, Mother, and Father appear to have everything well in hand. So I do not see any reason for me to cool my heels here, particularly when you are alone in London and undoubtedly doing nothing.

To that end, I am on my way to London to assist you in your search for a suitable spouse. I anticipate all of your complaints. Do spare me having to hear them.

John

FROM GAVIN HARTFORD
    8 Half Moon Street, London
TO CHARLES KENTWORTHY, ESQ.
    16 Berkeley Square, London

15 January 1816

KENTWORTHY,

Gerry sent me another spell. Would you like to attempt dinner and a casting again? Tomorrow evening, perhaps? I will endeavor to not get sick this time.

Hartford

FROM CHARLES KENTWORTHY, ESQ.
    16 Berkeley Square, London
TO GAVIN HARTFORD
    8 Half Moon Street, London

15 January 1816

MY DEAR GAVIN,

I would be delighted.

Charles

FROM GAVIN HARTFORD
    8 Half Moon Street, London
TO GERALDINE HARTFORD
    Shulfield Hall, Tutting-on-Cress

16 January 1816

GERRY,

A great deal has happened since I received your letter.

First, let me tell you that I did manage to ask Charles about his family. We had dinner at the club the other night and he told me all about it. His father died when he was very young. He was a bit vague on the details, but I gather his father was abroad when it happened. His mother died shortly after, due to an illness. He has no siblings, so this left him entirely alone. His aunt came to live with him after his mother's death, but apparently she was not fond of children, so he spent a great deal of his time at Viscount Finlington's estate. It was all rather sad, really, so I understand why he was not keen to discuss it. I feel as if I know him even better now, which is nice. Although I am still sorry that I did not think to ask him about it sooner.

Thank you for sending me another spell. I do appreciate it. I sent a message around to Charles as soon as I received it, inviting him to dinner and to watch the casting a second time. I promised him I would attempt to not get sick this time around and I'm pleased to report that I managed to fulfill this promise. Dinner was a livelier affair when Charles was not burdened with carrying the entire conversation by himself. I finally remembered to tell him of your appalling lack of faith in my judgment. He told me to assure you I said nothing untoward in our conversation with Finlington at Vauxhall Gardens.

After dinner, we withdrew to the drawing room and I cast the spell.

Since you were kind enough to find treated dragon's breath for the purpose, I am enclosing what I have left from what I purchased. It is untreated, as you likely know, so do take care. You will surely find more use for it than I will.

The spell was very well constructed, Gerry. We drank through an entire pot of tea at leisure and our tea was perfectly warm the entire time. My only note is that I think the counterspell could be simpler. Charles expressed a great deal of concern that I would burn my fingers when I tried to get my handkerchief to cool back down. I had a devil of a time getting him to let me proceed with the casting. I fear my illness has forever marred his opinion of my constitution.

After we finished the tea, I had a bottle of burgundy brought out. We shared a moment of comfortable quiet before he said, "Would you care to accompany me to Goring's tomorrow, my dear? There was a watch fob I was hoping to buy there. I should like to see if it is still available."

I looked at him in surprise. "You never went? I thought you meant to look ages ago."

"You were ill," he said. "I thought it better to wait until you were fully recovered before I suggested a trip across town. You know how I am with shopping. I like to spend the whole day on an excursion. I feared I might get carried away and exhaust you."

"You did not need me for the errand, surely."

"Of course not," he said, smiling. "But I wished for your company all the same."

This statement affected me in a way I cannot properly express. I felt a warmth in my chest I knew was not attributed to the wine.

"Will you wait here a moment?" I said.

He nodded, bemused.

I fetched the watch and fob at once. I got up in such haste, in fact, I forgot to set down my glass of wine and had to remember to take it back with me. As I returned to the drawing room, I felt a strange sense of nervousness and I stood on the threshold for a moment, hesitant.

He turned and looked at me. "Everything all right, darling?"

"Yes, perfectly," I said, shaking off the anxiety. I sat beside him on the sofa. "I wish to give you this. I bought it before my illness. The day I got caught in the rain, in fact. I've been meaning to give it to you. I'm sure I should have given it to you an age ago, but…well…here," I said, holding the watch and fob out.

He did not take them right away. Slowly, he set his glass of wine on the side table before he took them from my hand.

"Good heavens, Gavin," he breathed. "Why on earth—?"

"You wanted it," I said.

"I know," he said, with a laugh. "But I never expected… You did not need to buy it for me. Not to mention a watch to go with it."

"I had been wanting to purchase a gift for you for some time," I said. "But I was unsure what you would like. When you mentioned wanting this fob, I thought it would suit. Did I get the wrong one? Do you not like it?"

"Don't be silly, darling," he said, pressing my hand with his. "Of course I like it. I just do not know what I have done to deserve it."

"You paid my debt at Nesbit's," I said. "You bought me books of poetry. You looked after me when I fell ill. You took me out riding nearly every day. You got me invitations to balls and dinner parties. You pushed me to take up boxing. You—"

"You hate boxing," he interjected.

"Yes," I said. "But you have done so much for me, Charles. I can never repay you. And I…I don't know what I did to deserve your friendship." I looked at my hand, which was still clasped in his. "But I am grateful for it. I do not tell you enough how much…how much your friendship has meant to me."

He put his gift on the table next to his wine and reached up to brush the hair away from my face, still keeping his other hand clasped firmly around mine. "You did not need to buy it for me," he said, his voice soft. "I know it was a great expense." His hand slipped from my hair to cup my cheek, his thumb rubbing against my temple. "Do you really believe there to be a debt between us?"

I swallowed. "I am sure I must be a great trial to you. I have fought you at every step in our friendship. I do not know how you have put up with me."

"Did I not tell you once," he said, leaning forward a little, "that I love a good challenge?"

I was having a hard time breathing then. Perhaps because I was unnerved by having him so close to me. Or perhaps it was the wine. You know I never used to drink wine. I find wine far too heady and I have often avoided it. Although, I daresay I have had a great deal more of it since befriending Charles. In any case, I had so wanted to provide a better experience than the last time he had joined me for dinner, it seemed the most reasonable thing in the world for me to bring out a good bottle of wine. I was so caught up in noticing my shortness of breath, his close proximity, his thumb against my temple, our hands still clasped together, and vaguely remembering I still had a glass of wine in my other hand, that I could think of nothing to say to him in response. I simply stared at him.

Then, with no more warning than a small smile, he moved his hand from my cheek to the back of my neck, gently pulled me forward, and kissed me.

Is it improper for me to tell my little sister about a kiss I shared with another man? I daresay it is. I'm certain Mother would have the vapors if she knew. But then, she would likely have the vapors about many things we have discussed and that has never stopped us before. And you would probably curse me if I did not tell you everything. If I am wrong and you would rather not read this next bit, then do skip ahead to the next page or something and you can claim your innocent eyes are still intact, or some such rot.

I have never been kissed before, Gerry. It never struck me as a comfortable thing to do. Does one taste what the other person has recently eaten, for instance? When exactly are you supposed to breathe? Before? After? During? Are lips dry and rough? That hardly seems enjoyable. But wet lips do not seem appealing either. And I can honestly say I have never looked at Charles and imagined how his lips would feel. Do people really look at someone's lips and think of such things? I suppose some people must or we would never have started it up in the first place. At any rate, if it had been up to me, kissing would likely have never been discovered.

Kissing Charles was far more enjoyable than I could have imagined, had I thought to do so. His lips were not dry or rough or particularly wet. They were soft and there was sweetness from the wine on them still. I think it must have been on mine too, because I got the strangest sensation that he was tasting my lips, if you can countenance it. Then, just when I was beginning to get accustomed to the whole thing, he pulled away.

He studied my face for a moment before saying, "I have been wanting to do that since the night we met at Nesbit's."

"Not really?" I said.

"Ever since you read me a scold for paying your gaming debt."

"But I was so very drunk."

He laughed. "You were. And completely adorable."

I wrinkled my nose. "I'm glad you never said as much to me then. And I don't believe you anyway. I was a horrid grump."

"Yes," he said. "I was intrigued. I had seen you at the club many times before, but you were always so reserved and kept entirely to yourself. I wanted to know what made you get soused and then I wondered what you were so afraid of."

I suddenly remembered I still had a drink in my hand. I looked at it and was relieved to see it had not spilled. Slowly, I placed it on the side table, careful not to break contact with Charles. Even as I did it, I wondered at my own caution. All I can say by way of explanation, Gerry, is his presence felt uniquely comforting. I was not in a hurry to lose it.

"I do not remember being afraid of anything," I said as I looked back at him.

He was smiling at me in that amused way of his. I suppose I must have looked a little silly in carefully setting my glass aside. "You were without realizing it, I think," he said. The hand at the back of my neck moved to brush through my hair before settling back in place.

"And what, pray, do you think I was afraid of?"

"Now that I know you? I think you were afraid of your own audacity to get drunk. You were afraid of London. You were afraid of your own loneliness. You were afraid of my attention. You were afraid of me," he said.

I scoffed. "Stuff."

He laughed and kissed me again, briefly this time. I barely had time to register and kiss him back before he was pulling away again. He stroked my cheek. "You are very dear to me, you know," he said.

I was trying to come up with a reply for this when I heard the front door open and the butler said, "Mr. Hartford, what a pleasant surprise to see you, sir."

Before I could wonder who was at the door, Charles had pulled away from me and was busy scooping up the watch and fob in one hand and his glass of burgundy in the other. I was still sitting, gaping like a guppy when John walked in the door.

"Good God, John," I said, standing up. "What the devil are you doing here?"

John gave me that imperious look he gets when he's in a bad mood. He looked Charles briefly up and down and said, "Won't you introduce me to your friend, Gav?"

"Oh," I said. "Yes, of course. This is Charles...Kentworthy. Er—my brother John."

It was hardly an eloquent introduction. But, you see, I realized I had started calling Charles by his first name for the later part of the evening. I felt a strange reluctance to revert back to the usual formality.

Charles stood and gave John a neat little bow. "A pleasure, Mr. Hartford."

John returned it with his usual stiffness. "Charmed, I'm sure. I hope you will excuse my brother, Mr. Kentworthy. Clearly, months in London were not sufficient to teach him proper behavior and correct address."

"What are you doing here?" I said again, which of course proved John right, confound it.

"Didn't you receive my letter?"

The fact is, Gerry, I did receive his letter, but I didn't read it. It was the first letter he sent that I decided to ignore. John rolled his eyes and went to the table in the front hall where the mail is always placed. He strode back into the room, waving his own unopened letter at me.

"Now I know why you haven't been responding to my letters," he said. "I came to help you, of course. I've explained it perfectly well in here. I am in no mood to repeat myself." He tossed it on the table next to the wine. "Besides, why shouldn't I look in on my little brother? You are, in a manner of speaking, my responsibility."

"Rubbish," I said. "I am no such thing. You are tired of the infant already, aren't you? Or is it Veronica you're hiding from?"

John did not answer me but picked up the bottle of burgundy. I expected him to make some slighting remark about me dipping into the good bottles but, surprisingly, he simply returned it to the table and looked down at us—which was no small feat considering Charles is taller than John.

"Well, I'm sure you both have much to talk about," Charles said after a moment. "I would not like to be in the way. Good night, Mr. Hartford. It was a pleasure meeting you. Good night, Gavin," he said to me. He inclined his head to both of us, and I saw him pocket the watch and fob when he turned to me.

I was relieved he was still calling me by my first name. I was also a little relieved he did not call me "my dear" or "darling" in front of John. He must have realized John would not approve. I wanted to walk him to the door, but he left the room in too much haste.

As soon as the door clicked shut behind Charles, John said, "You should not associate yourself with someone like Charles Kentworthy."

I turned to him. "And why is that, pray?"

"He is a bad influence."

"Stuff."

He snorted. "You never drink. Yet I come in to find you drinking burgundy of all things. He addresses you by your first name. You were sitting alone with the man with no chaperone. You were occupying the same sofa—"

"And why should that signify?"

"Because," he said, lowering his voice as if Charles was still present, "people of Kentworthy's reputation should be treated with caution."

"What are you doing here?" I said. This must have been the third or fourth time I had asked him.

"Do I need an excuse to visit our house in town?"

"Yes, you jolly well do," I said. "When you have a child only recently born."

"Do you have any idea how much infants cry, Gav?" He pinched the bridge of his nose in that way he does when he thinks he is explaining something that should be obvious.

"Yes, and it is precisely why I never intend to have them."

He scoffed. "Don't talk nonsense."

I did not reply.

"I wrote you four letters," he said. "You did not reply to a single one. Veronica sent out a dozen requests to have you invited places. You rejected all of the invitations. Now, I will admit you were sent here without preparation, but why not at least ask for help? I could easily forgive your reticence to socialize if you simply admitted to your faults, but you have ignored all of my well-intentioned advice. You are ungrateful. You are churlish. You are impolite. You are ill-humored. And you have no sense of responsibility," he said, pacing in front of me. "It is high time you grew up and thought about your future."

"I don't see why you're in such a state about it. Mother and Father don't seem to mind."

"Yes, well," he said. "Our parents give you far too much credit, I think. You were given free rein in London, and you managed to befriend only one person, and he happens to be one of the most disreputable rakes in the country. You are clearly unfit to handle your own affairs." He sighed. "I worry about you, Gav. I truly do. What do you intend to do as you get older? You will certainly not be able to continue sitting around as you've been doing."

"I have not been sitting around," I protested. "And you had no call to come all the way down here just—"

"I really am far too tired to hear your arguments just now," he said. "Do spare me your usual churlishness. I am off to bed." He walked past me. "We will call on Veronica's parents after breakfast. They will surely wish to know how the infant is doing."

"I have an appointment after breakfast."

He paused at the door. "And what appointment might that be?"

"I'm to meet Kentworthy at Hyde Park. We are to go riding."

"I think he will understand you breaking it for a family obligation."

"They're not my family, John."

He sighed. "Very well," he said. "But I would like it to be the last appointment you keep with the man. Do you understand?" Before I could answer, he added, "I know you did not bring your horse to town. Don't tell me you purchased one during your stay."

"Kentworthy has been kind enough to let me use one of his."

He stared at me for a moment. "Do you have any idea— no, never mind. You evidently don't. I forbid you from using his horses in the future."

"What—"

"If you wish to keep your appointment with him, you can walk through the park. I am sure he will understand."

Before I could respond, he left the room. I stood still for several minutes, with my heart hammering in my chest and my hands shaking. It seemed impossible that so much had happened in such a short space of time. I ran a hand through my hair and was reminded of the way Charles did that very thing. I let out a deep breath and finished off both glasses of burgundy.

I then wrote out a note for Charles to be sent out in the morning. I did not cancel my appointment with him, of course. Nor do I have any intention of listening to John's nonsense about Charles being a bad influence. But I did wish to warn him that he would not find the house quite as hospitable until John quit it.

I advise you not to send me any more spells in the meantime. I will most certainly keep you informed.

Also, I would very much like to visit for the wedding. Please let me know when the date is settled. I will ask Charles if he wishes to accompany me, but I might wait until John has left and everything is back to normal.

Affectionately,

Gavin

P.S. I ended up writing to Charles for advice on the callers. He actually wrote to the Dukex of Molbury on my behalf and they instructed me to not accept callers without a chaperone, specifically people with whom I was not already acquainted. It has been a nuisance to hear people at the door for several hours a day, but I am glad to know I can avoid such interactions for reasons of propriety.

FROM GAVIN HARTFORD
8 Half Moon Street, London
TO CHARLES KENTWORTHY, ESQ.
16 Berkeley Square, London

17 January 1816

CHARLES,

Please allow me to apologize for my brother's behavior. You can probably see why I have never spoken of John in affectionate terms. I will tell you all about him when we meet in the park. He has taken it into his head that you will prove a bad influence over me and requested I break off our engagement so we may visit his dull in-laws. I put him off, of course. But John can be thoroughly disagreeable, so I do not know if it will be wise to continue in our usual routine while he is here. Particularly if he has decided he has a right to fill up my time with his own commitments.

He has also forbidden me from using your horses. I do not know why he finds your generosity so objectionable. Normally, I wouldn't give a fig for John's wishes, but he will make things dashed uncomfortable if he isn't heeded. I suppose using your horses is one battle I need not fight with my brother. At least, not until I have a better idea of how long he means to stay here. I hope you will not be opposed to simply walking in the park tomorrow.

Gavin

· · ·

From Charles Kentworthy, Esq.
  16 Berkeley Square, London
To Gavin Hartford
  8 Half Moon Street, London

17 January 1816

My dear Gavin,

Please do not think a thing of it, darling. You are not responsible for your brother's actions. I daresay if he had entered the room a moment sooner, he would have been completely convinced of my bad influence over you. I hope you will forgive me for my abrupt departure. Your brother did not seem in the mood to entertain. Besides, he had been travelling and I was sure he wished to rest.

As it happens, my aunt has been requesting my presence in Bath. Perhaps it would be a good time for me to heed her summons? I shall stay a week at most, my dear. Hopefully, by the time I return, your brother will either have left or will have relaxed in his protestations.

I will see you shortly. Please do not fret about the horses; I am quite happy to walk instead.

Charles

From Geraldine Hartford
  Shulfield Hall, Tutting-on-Cress
To Gavin Hartford
  8 Half Moon Street, London

19 January 1816

Dear Gavin,

How dare John? How dare he leave his wife with a new child? How dare he leave our parents with his horrid wife and new child? How dare he impose on you in such a manner? And tell you who you can be friends with? It is perfectly outrageous. And how dare he speak slightingly of dear Charles who has been the best friend you could ask for? It is the outside of enough. I have half a mind to go down to London and tell him off. Shall I do it, Gavin? You know I would if you asked me to.

Up until you detailed John's arrival, I was in raptures at your letter. He loves you, Gavin! I knew how it must be! I think in your own way, you might love him back. I do hope so. He is quite the best thing that has ever happened to you. I hope you two shall marry and then you must allow me to come visit you. I feel as if I know Charles already and I am eager to meet him. You should find a way to roust John and send him back home. Remind him of his duties. Lord knows he does that often enough with us. I will write to Mama and see if I can hint that John ought to return home.

I hope your next letter tells me all about how John has left and Charles has taken you back in his arms. Allow me my romanticism, Gavin.

Affectionately,

Gerry

P.S. I am a little miffed John managed to meet Charles before I did. I will never forgive you if I'm the last one to meet him.

P.P.S. Thank you for sending me the dragon's breath. I will most certainly make good use of it. Clever of you to send it out before John noticed.

P.P.P.S. Has your hair grown significantly since I last saw you? It sounds as if Charles sweeps hair from your forehead quite a bit. I would advise you not to cut it as he seems to enjoy it. But I am surprised Mama did not see it cut when she was there.

• • •

FROM CHARLES KENTWORTHY, ESQ.
11 Royal Crescent, Bath
TO GAVIN HARTFORD
8 Half Moon Street, London

20 January 1816

MY DEAR GAVIN,

How are you faring? Bath is perfectly lovely, but I find myself missing London too much to enjoy it. I wish we had been granted more time before your brother arrived and before I departed. I feel there was a great deal left to be said. Did I ever thank you properly for the watch fob, dear? I fear I was too overwhelmed when you presented it to me to give you adequate thanks. It is the only one I ever wear now.

My aunt has planned a dinner party for me next week, so I am afraid I shall have to delay my return until afterwards. I am sorry, my darling. I promised to be gone a week and I hate to go back on my word.

Is your brother still in town? Has he indicated how long he intends to stay? I am sure his wife cannot appreciate being abandoned in such a way. Is he still being horrid to you or has he relented now that I am gone from London? I hope he does not always speak to you in that cold manner and that his attitude was merely for my benefit.

I feel I am finally beginning to understand why you have such a dreadful tendency to speak ill of yourself. Please do not put too much stock in your brother's opinion of your character. You behave charmingly, dearest, and have beautiful address.

I will send you a note when I return, unless my return is delayed again, in which case I will write to you from here.

I hope you are surviving well enough and that your brother leaves soon.

Affectionately,

Charles

P.S. Please give my regards to your sister. Have you apprised her of the situation? I would dearly like to know what she thinks of all of this.

FROM GAVIN HARTFORD
8 Half Moon Street, London
TO GERALDINE HARTFORD
Shulfield Hall, Tutting-on-Cress

21 January 1816

GERRY,

I hate to disappoint you, but John is still in London and driving me to distraction. And Charles has gone to Bath. He left because his aunt requested he visit her there and he thought it prudent to quit London for the time being, what with John in town. I confess to feeling bereft at his departure. It is stupid and pathetic. God knows I am not lonely right now; John does not allow me to be. He has dragged me to every social commitment he has made for himself and it is all a great bore. His friends are unpardonably dull.

After he failed to convince me to break off my appointment at the park with Charles, John then accompanied me when I went. It was galling. Charles and I were forced to discuss platitudes. John completely integrated himself into the conversation and kept it from being interesting. I had hoped to have a final conversation with Charles before he left. Perhaps discuss what had passed between us the night before. Hint that I might miss him. Apologize about John. But of course I could not say any of these things with John breathing down my neck. I could write it all in a letter, I suppose. But some things do not seem fitting for a letter.

Also, I am no longer able to avoid the callers. His first day here, John heard someone at the door when we were taking tea and said, "Who is that?"

"I'm sure I don't know," I said. "Probably just a social call. I've had no end of them for the past week. But I was told by a reliable source that I could not accept them without a chaperone." I confess I said this a little smugly. "So, the butler has been telling them I'm not at home."

Then John said, just as smugly, "Well, you have a chaperone now." He summoned the butler and, to my horror, told him to accept all callers from that point on.

It has been dreadful, Gerry. I am forced to sit and make small talk with people. And anytime we miss them, we are compelled to call on *them*. What a ghastly rule. I can only hope it dissipates soon.

Do you remember Veronica's horrid brother, Alistair Hampstead? Well, John has taken it into his head to foist Hampstead upon me, claiming I need better influences in my social sphere. He is forever inviting the blasted man to join us at dinner or in the card room at Nesbit's. I detest him. He manages to be even more condescending than John and he keeps calling me "little Hartford" as if I were not a fully grown man.

At all times, John is reading me a lecture on proper behavior: how I ought to be paying more attention to this person or that person, how I was too curt, how I do not speak enough, how I speak too much on the wrong subject. Would you believe he took exception to the way I tied my cravat? He said it was too frivolous and was "evidence of Kentworthy's damaging influence." I confess I have tied my cravat in that exact style ever since, simply to annoy him. It is not even my favorite knot as it takes a long time to do and ruffles under my chin in an irritating way. It is absurd, of course, to suffer such things in order to annoy my brother. But then, John has always had that effect on me. I'm beginning to see why Mother sent me away in the first place.

I have also started boxing nearly every day. John does not approve of boxing as he finds it vulgar and thinks I ought to focus on my fencing. This is another thing I have taken to doing simply to annoy him. As it is a perfectly respectable pastime, he cannot keep me from it. He knows very well our parents would only encourage me to be doing something other than holing up in the library. It felt punishing at first, but I find I am beginning to enjoy it. I spend all of my time feeling tense and irritable around John and then I am free to release everything when I box. I have not admitted all of this to Charles, but I intend to. I am sure it will make him laugh.

I was able to sneak away from John once. I complained of a headache while at a dinner party. Since we were in mixed company, he could not tell me off for it or scold me for lying. The hostess was very sympathetic. I managed to persuade her I needed a bit of fresh air and was so convincingly apologetic about ruining the evening that she took my side of things when I told John he should remain and enjoy the party. I knew John wouldn't stay behind long, so I immediately hailed a hackney and told the driver to go in any direction but quickly. Then, I sat back and tried to think of a place where I might go where John wouldn't find me and I could get at least some reprieve. Nesbit's was out of the question, of course, and the townhouse was the first place John would look. I had half a mind to go to Viscount Finlington's house, but I don't know him so well as to barge in uninvited, so I did the next best thing I could think of and directed the driver to take me to Covent Garden.

I felt foolish for the decision the moment I arrived. But the prospect of going back to get lectured at by John was far more grim than traversing through Covent Garden alone, so I paid the driver and strode into the crowd. I did not, of course, have any intention of actually hiring someone. But it was nice to be in a crowd of people, knowing John could not possibly find me. When a voice hailed me from the side and I turned to see Mr. Bowles approaching, well, I was dashed relieved.

"I didn't expect to see you again," he said, smiling at me. He leaned down and kissed my cheek. "Stopping by for a visit?"

"I'm trying to avoid an unpleasant relation," I admitted.

He laughed. "I can certainly help with that. What happened to Mr. Kentworthy?"

"He went to Bath," I said. "In part to avoid this same relation. I'm not sure when he'll be back."

He took my hand. "Come on. Let's get you a drink. You look like you need it."

He took me to a pub. It was a very seedy sort of place, honestly. Under normal circumstances, I would be quite nervous to go in, much less accompanied by someone like Mr. Bowles. But I did feel a small thrill at the rebelliousness of it all. I insisted on paying for our drinks, which seemed to please him. He handed me a pint of ale and then took me to a booth in the corner of the pub. Considering how I could barely look at Mr. Bowles the first time we met, I am shocked now to realize I didn't panic, not even when he sat beside me on the bench.

"So," he said, after taking a sip of ale. "What has you running to this side of town, eh? Tell old Lino everything."

It was funny to hear him refer to himself in such a way. I had a better look at him during this encounter, and I rather think he is younger than I am, for all his wisdom. I did as he asked—starting, I should add, with a description of the trip to Peerless Pond, which had him laughing out loud.

"Bless me," he said. "You really did take my advice to heart, didn't you?"

When I nodded, he ruffled my hair and told me to keep going. I told him about how I bought Charles the watch and fob, about my illness, about the ball, about the night Charles kissed me and John arrived, and concluded with Charles's subsequent departure and my personal torture at the hands of our brother.

After I was finished, Mr. Bowles gave an expressive sort of whistle and took a large drink from his pint. Then he nodded to mine and said, "Drink up. You've barely touched it. Don't you know a proper vintage when you see one?"

I laughed and did as he advised.

"Now that's more like it," he said. "And a pretty smile it is too."

I blushed at this and took another sip of ale.

He grinned. "So, what comes next?"

"What do you mean?"

"When he comes back, what will you do?"

"Oh," I said. "I'm not sure. I feel as though I have a great deal to tell him."

"That you do," he said, with a nod. "But if I know you at all, you'll get yourself all flustered if you don't plan out what you'd like to say when he returns. Best to have it worked out now."

I was a little shocked that he should have my measure so completely. I could think of nothing to say in reply.

He tutted and cupped my chin gently. "Do you remember what I told you the first time we met?"

"You said I was too serious by half."

He gave me a rueful smile and stroked my cheek with his thumb. "Dear me. I really got under your skin, didn't I?"

"Only because you were right," I said. "I cannot think why Charles would choose me. He could have anyone and he's been spending all his time with a grumpy sod who's afraid of his own shadow half the time."

"Now, I never said that."

"I know you didn't. I did."

He framed my face with his hands, much like he had done the first night we met. "My advice was to be bold. You've gone and done it, haven't you? You jumped, you danced, you gave. And now, when he comes back, you'll have to be bold again. I reckon you know exactly what you need to say, only you're terrified of having to say it."

I took a deep breath. "Isn't everyone?"

He chuckled. "Of course they are, my pretty buck. But it's the bold ones who say the words anyway."

"You're right. Thank you, Mr. Bowles."

He blew a raspberry and said, "Stop addressing me like I'm respectable."

"Sorry, Lino."

He turned my face and kissed my cheek. "That's more like it. Now finish up your drink, there's a good lad. And then you'd better get back before that brother of yours sends out the whole constabulary."

Naturally, when I finally got home, John read me a fine scold about leaving prematurely and then disappearing, and then coming back smelling like, well, a pub. So he hasn't let me out of his sight ever since, except when I'm boxing. Even then, I'm quite sure he has friends at Muller's who keep an eye on me. But I have to tell you, Gerry, it was worth it. Lino is right: I know what I will say to Charles. It is just a matter of being bold enough to say it.

It suddenly occurs to me that I ought to have paid Lino for spending time with me, albeit just for conversation. He never mentioned it, so I did not think of it until now. I hope I did not cost him customers or anything. Now it would be well nigh impossible for me to get back to him in order to rectify the situation. I can hardly tell John about it. Bother. I have been a shabby friend to him too, haven't I? Perhaps Charles will be able to assist when he returns.

Lest you complain again that I have neglected to describe someone who you are unlikely to ever meet, Lino is about average height, a good head or so taller than I am, and very slender. He has light brown skin and a mop of dark curly hair. He has dark eyes that are framed with long eyelashes. He is an angular sort of person with a narrow face and sharp features. He also has freckles, which I found somewhat incongruous to his overall striking appearance, but I suppose one cannot control such things.

I am relieved I did not wholly scandalize you with the details of my previous letter. But I wish you would not describe Charles and I as if we were characters in a tawdry book. Imagine Charles taking me up in his arms. It is an absurd image. I am sure he would never do such a sentimental thing.

Affectionately,

Gavin

P.S. I have read over my letter and I wish to apologize for being so contrary, particularly in that last paragraph. I have no excuse except to say that John is driving me out of my mind. I would to God Charles could come back from Bath. It has hardly been a week since he left and yet I am too aware of his absence in my daily life.

P.P.S. Yes, my hair has grown quite long. It curls over my forehead and ears and, to my mind, looks a little disheveled. Charles has told me in the past that tousled hair is fashionable and many men yearn to have hair that waves as becomingly as mine does. I typically find it a great nuisance, but I'm not sure I mind it anymore. Mother did comment on it when she was in town but she was too concerned about my health at the time to persuade me to get it cut. I should state, however, that John did his level best. He told me I looked "absurdly mussed." I informed him it was perfectly fashionable. If I hadn't already grown accustomed to it, I daresay it would be yet another thing I had decided to like simply because John took offense to it.

FROM GAVIN HARTFORD
  8 Half Moon Street, London
TO CHARLES KENTWORTHY, ESQ.
  11 Royal Crescent, Bath

22 January 1816

CHARLES,

I am glad you are enjoying your time in Bath, but I would vastly prefer it if you were in London and John were home where he ought to be. Yes, he is still here and I wish him to perdition. I know I always complained about the busy schedule you imposed on me, but I must say your schedule was at least enjoyable and varied. John merely drags me around to all of his social calls and invitations. It is abominably dull. His friends are dreadful, truly. He has even insisted on accepting every social call we've had (those still haven't stopped). So every day I am forced to sit and talk to strangers. I suppose some of them are no longer strangers now, but it is still abominable.

And yes, he is still being horrid. I have resorted to boxing in order to avoid his company, if you can believe it. I am still dreadful at it, but it is the one place where John has not followed me, so it has become an unexpected sort of haven. In fact, when you do come back to London, it might be the best place for you to find me. Then you will be saved from John's company. Unfortunately, I've seen several of his friends there, so we will not be able to avoid them.

I would urge you to return sooner, but John has taken complete control of my social engagements. I'm sure I could not bear to know you were in town and that I was not permitted to see you. I suppose I really was fortunate to have the freedom to do as I wished for months. I do not like having a chaperone one jot. I know it is the done thing and I daresay the Dukex of Molbury would be pleased by this turn of events, but I would hope even they would recognize how miserable John is making me with his presence. I do not remember being so frustrated back at home when I was with my family for social gatherings. So I cannot determine if all chaperones are dreadful or if it is simply John who is dreadful.

I did manage to sneak away from his company the other night and went to the first place I could think of where he wouldn't find me. This turned out to be Covent Garden and I had a nice chat with your friend, Mr. Bowles. Does that surprise you? Well, it surprised me too. At any rate, John no longer trusts me an inch. Not that he did before.

I did tell Gerry and she is furious about John being here. She has threatened to set my mother on him. With the way he has been behaving since he arrived in London, I daresay he deserves it.

I shall keep you informed of any changes to my circumstances.

Sincerely,

Gavin

P.S. I probably ought to clarify that when I say I had a chat with Mr. Bowles, it really was just a chat. I should hate for you to get the wrong impression. It occurred to me afterwards that our conversation might have cost Mr. Bowles valuable time with potential customers. Ought I have paid him for his time? I am unfamiliar with such protocols. I would hate to learn I essentially stole from the man.

FROM SEBASTIAN HARTFORD
Digory College, Oxford
TO GAVIN HARTFORD
8 Half Moon Street, London

23 January 1816

WHAT HO, GAVIN!

I just heard the most shocking bit of news! Everard Morningcroft just got back from London—his sister was being presented and he got to visit for a week, lucky devil—and he says he was at a ball held by Lord and Lady Such-and-Such. Frankly, I don't remember the details. At any rate, he says he saw Mr. Charles Kentworthy, Esquire, dancing with a young man who looked quite remarkably like me. And he says he saw it happen twice!

Gavin! Do you mean to tell me you stood up with Mr. Kentworthy at a ball in London? What a turn up! Imagine you doing such a thing!

I don't mean to suggest that I'm surprised to learn your friendship with Kentworthy is more than you have indicated. I distinctly remember how much you stared at Arthur Cunningham, even if he was too busy staring at Gerry to notice your interest. I confess I have always been secretly pleased at the knowledge that you and I are alike in that way. But I am astonished that you have changed so much as to actually do something about it. It is very unlike you. And dancing twice with the same gentleman? From you, that's practically a declaration!

Do write back to confirm this bit of gossip. And tell me when you and Mr. Kentworthy are to be married. And then please send for me so I can meet him and he can introduce me to interesting people.

Affectionately,
Seb

P.S. I most certainly would not prefer being tutored at home. And I beg you to not put such a ghastly idea into Father's head. Do you wish to torture me? A tutor? Really? Are you barmy?

FROM CHARLES KENTWORTHY, ESQ.
   11 Royal Crescent, Bath
To GAVIN HARTFORD
   8 Half Moon Street, London

24 January 1816

MY DEAR GAVIN,

I was distressed to learn that your brother is making you miserable. So I hope you will not be angry with me when I confess I have asked Bertie to keep an eye on you while I am away. You will likely receive an invitation to dine with him in the next day or two. Knowing Bertie, he may invite your brother along out of politeness, out of propriety, and also out of curiosity. He is an adroit conversationalist, so I trust him to keep the conversation from being unpleasant. I have also warned him off talking about your sister's spell-building proclivities in front of your brother. I hazard a guess it is something neither of you would like him to know.

I daresay the dukex will be relieved to learn of your brother's arrival, but if they knew you were unhappy in the situation, there is a very good chance they would intervene. I do not know if the dukex's intervention would put you more at ease or not, so I will wait upon your reply before soliciting their help as well.

It is strange to be in Bath while you are still in London. I confess I do not like this distance between us. You should come to Bath with me next time. We will take the waters and see the concerts. I will translate every opera for you, if you wish it. My aunt will adore you.

Affectionately,

Charles

P.S. I am all curiosity about your conversation with Lino. Do not fret about the money. He would have explained such terms in advance if he expected payment. However, I will look in on him upon my return to London to ensure he is not hurting financially from the interaction.

FROM GERALDINE HARTFORD
   Shulfield Hall, Tutting-on-Cress
TO GAVIN HARTFORD
   8 Half Moon Street, London

25 January 1816

DEAR GAVIN,

I wrote to Mama and she is not pleased at John's behavior. Apparently, he didn't tell anyone where he was going or what he was doing. He merely said he was taking care of some business interests and would return within a month or two. Veronica has been beside herself at having been left like that. For once, I cannot blame her. It was a shocking thing for John to do. He is not only making her suffer, he is punishing everyone else as well for you know they have had to suffer through her temper. Hopefully, either Mama or Papa will send for him and then he will have to go back.

As soon as John leaves, you must write to Charles and invite him back to London. You are getting moody again and I think Charles and I are the only ones who can cure you of it. I would come, but we both know you would prefer his company right now.

God keep you from Alistair Hampstead. Odious man. I

detest him. Every time I have been in his company, he has leered at me in the most horrid way. I cannot believe John would think Alistair Hampstead to be superior company to Charles Kentworthy. Regardless of his reputation, Charles comes from a very good family. John is a fool to dislike him so. Hopefully when John leaves, you can avoid Mr. Hampstead's company too.

I am pleased to hear you received another good dose of sense from Mr. Bowles. It really is wonderful how much your friendship with Charles has opened you up to more friendships in general. I daresay our parents and John would not strictly approve of Mr. Bowles as a friend, but I think his kindness and intelligence do much to recommend him.

As to the matter of his payment, I'm sure Charles would be a better person to ask. I haven't the faintest idea about the rules of etiquette in such situations.

Do tell me if you need me to come save you. And do tell me if Charles comes and saves you, which would be even better.

Affectionately,
Gerry

FROM THE RIGHT HONORABLE VISCOUNT BERTRAM **Beauregard Aubrey Finlington**
   12 Berkeley Square, London
TO GAVIN HARTFORD
   8 Half Moon Street, London

26 January 1816

DEAR MR. HARTFORD,

I trust Charlie told you that he asked me to check in and see how you are weathering your current guest. I would be delighted if you would join me for dinner tomorrow night. I do apologize, m'dear, for the last-minute invitation.

If your brother is disinclined to allow you to go alone, he is most certainly welcome to join. If you succeed in coming without him, so much the better.

I do have a prior engagement tonight. However, if you need a haven from the current storm that is unpleasant relations (trust me, darling, I have some myself), you are more than welcome to come to my house, whether I am present or not. I shall instruct my butler to let you in at any time.

Cordially,
Bertie Finlington

FROM GAVIN HARTFORD
8 Half Moon Street, London
TO THE RIGHT HONORABLE VISCOUNT BERTRAM BEAUREGARD
Aubrey Finlington
12 Berkeley Square, London

26 January 1816

MY LORD,

Charles did inform me that he had sent word to you to look in on me. I most certainly appreciate the invitation. My brother was not best pleased to hear that I had plans tomorrow (I confess, I pretended we had a prior engagement and it had slipped my mind), but your name carried too much weight for him to put up a lot of fuss.

He is, thankfully, already committed to another event, so he will not be joining us. But he did express a desire to meet you so he will be accompanying me to your house before going to his own engagement. You may well wonder why my brother insists on escorting me to a social call; I gave him the slip a few days ago so he no longer permits me to go about town alone. Appalling lack of trust, really, but then, that's my brother for you. It is for this reason that I am unlikely to take advantage of your generous offer to use your house, but I do hope you know I greatly appreciate it.

Sincerely,
Gavin Hartford

FROM THE RIGHT HONORABLE VISCOUNT BERTRAM
Beauregard Aubrey Finlington
   12 Berkeley Square, London
TO GAVIN HARTFORD
   8 Half Moon Street, London

26 January 1816

DEAR MR. HARTFORD,

I confess, my sweet, that I am all curiosity as to how you "gave him the slip." I do hope you know I intend to ask for all of the details. Dinner will be served at seven, but you will be welcome to come at any time. I am at your disposal, darling. As far as I am concerned, you may tell your brother I dine at the highly unfashionable hour of five. From what Charlie has described, I'd wager such a detail would bring me up in your brother's estimation.

Cordially,
Bertie Finlington

FROM GAVIN HARTFORD
  8 Half Moon Street, London
TO CHARLES KENTWORTHY, ESQ.
  11 Royal Crescent, Bath

26 January 1816

DEAR CHARLES,

I almost did not include the "dear" but I felt you would appreciate it, so I decided to add it. I tend to come to conclusions by circuitous ways. The past week without you has made a few things clear that had me muddled before. I cannot convey all of it properly in a letter, so I suppose it shall have to wait.

Viscount Finlington did invite me to dinner, as you predicted. He was very kind about it. I only hope I don't continue to make a fool of myself. I have never admitted it to you, Charles, but the gentleman really does make me frightfully nervous. I haven't the faintest idea why. I confess I was very nervous of you when we first met as well. But that was, frankly, for somewhat different reasons.

In any case, here's hoping I manage to actually talk to him when I go to dinner tomorrow night. John will not be joining us; he had a prior commitment and did not think it would be proper for us both to change our plans at the last minute. Thank God for that. Although he does plan to accompany me to his lordship's door in order to meet him. I suspect he wants to know where the viscount lives as well, if I'm honest.

Thank you for your assurances regarding my conversation with Mr. Bowles. If you do pay him for the time he spent with me, please tell me so I can repay you. What an absurd request that is. I cannot tell if retracting it would be worse, however, so I shall let it stand.

I should very much like to go to Bath with you sometime. Perhaps in the spring I can take you to visit my family as well. We can go riding across the estate. If we visit when Gerry is at home, the three of us can go riding together. It is beautiful in the mornings.

It is perfectly selfish of me to say this, I realize, but I hope you will not have to delay your trip again. It will not be easy to enjoy ourselves with my brother here, but London is not the same without you.

Yrs,

Gavin

FROM GAVIN HARTFORD
   8 Half Moon Street, London
TO SEBASTIAN HARTFORD
   Digory College, Oxford

27 January 1816

SEB,

I will not deny that I danced with Charles at the ball. Nor will I deny that I am fond of the gentleman. Beyond that, I have nothing else to declare.

I confess I am surprised to learn you suspected my persuasion. Particularly since you have never commented on it. Quite frankly, you astonish me.

On the subject of you coming to London, I don't know how many times I must tell you I am not the one you should be asking. That decision is entirely Father's and you know as well as I do what he will say. Although, in point of fact, John is here now and I would vastly prefer your company to his.

I hope you are well. Please try to keep out of trouble.

Affectionately,

Gavin

P.S. I notice that you did not actually deny my concerns. If I were not so busy suffering under John's company, I could spare some time to force a real answer from you. As it is, if you do not write back to me and tell me you are happy there, I will write to Father and ask him to winkle out the truth.

FROM GAVIN HARTFORD
8 Half Moon Street, London
TO GERALDINE HARTFORD
Shulfield Hall, Tutting-on-Cress

28 January 1816

GERRY,

John is still in town. Charles is still in Bath. It is all still exasperating, although I confess I have had a few unexpected reprieves.

I have already told you how John has insisted on accepting all social calls. I told Charles about it and I think he must have mentioned it to some people because several of my acquaintances have called since I sent him my letter. Lady and Lord Partridge came by, which was very nice. They were both shockingly eloquent about my "many charms." I think John was just as surprised as I was. I'm sure Charles put them up to it.

Miss Cartright and her mother called as well. John was extremely curious about how I had come to know them. I fear he may have misconstrued our friendship as a potential marriage prospect.

We missed a call from the Dukex of Molbury. Which, of course, meant we had to go call on them yesterday. I was frightfully nervous. I mean to say, their townhouse is practically palatial. John was just as nervous as I was, which ought to have made me feel better. Only it didn't, because then I was worried he might say something stupid.

The dukex was exactly as polite and intimidating as they

were at the ball. I introduced John and then we both kissed their hand. After we sat down, they said, "I am relieved to see you now have a chaperone, Mr. Hartford."

I did not know what to say to that since I couldn't very well admit I resented John for coming.

"I have never been easy with Gavin staying in London alone," John said.

"Your brother told me you recently had a baby. May I offer my felicitations?"

John blushed. "You are too kind, Your Grace."

"I am surprised your wife and child are well enough to travel so soon."

"I came here alone, Your Grace, to see to Gavin's prospects."

The dukex's eyes narrowed slightly. "Indeed? What an interesting family you are, to be sure."

John had the grace to look a little embarrassed. "It is unusual. But, as I said, I've been uneasy with Gavin's situation for months. Neither of my parents seemed concerned, so I knew they were unlikely to come and assist him. I can assure you my wife and child are in good hands back at home."

The dukex was silent for a long moment. Finally, they said, "I can certainly appreciate your uneasiness on your brother's behalf. It is most irregular for a younger sibling to be in London alone."

"Thank you," John said.

"However," the dukex continued. "I dislike the notion that you are the only person available to help him. You have your own family to take care of, Mr. Hartford."

John blushed again and said, "Yes, Your Grace. But I consider my younger siblings my responsibility as well."

They tilted their head in agreement. "Your concern does you credit, young man. They are your responsibility, in a manner of speaking. When your father dies, any unmarried and underage siblings will most certainly answer to you as head of the family. But you are not without friends, either of you. Mr. Hartford—or perhaps I should say, Mr. Gavin—requires a chaperone, but it need not be a relation. It is not uncommon for a friend of the family to take on the role."

John seemed to consider this. "I suppose I could ask my in-laws to—"

I couldn't stifle a groan before he finished the sentence. He glared at me.

I need hardly tell you, Gerry, that I'd prefer to have John as my chaperone than Mr. and Mrs. Hampstead. And that is saying something.

Fortunately, the dukex intervened before John could scold me. "They certainly pose one solution, yes. I might add that you have several possible options. I understand your brother is acquainted with Lady and Lord Partridge. I am sure they would be delighted to assist."

"Oh," John said. "Perhaps. I did meet them yesterday. But I confess I would prefer to leave him in the hands of someone I know better."

The dukex smiled a little. "Indeed, Mr. Hartford. Then might I also suggest that I would be glad to help as well?"

I was stunned. John must have been too, for he said, "Why?" And then hastily added, "That is, you are too kind, Your Grace. But we couldn't impose—"

"It would be no imposition, Mr. Hartford. As to why, I daresay you do not give your brother proper credit. I am sure we will get along very well. But, as we have just met, I do not wish to make you uneasy with my offer. So, let us agree to meet more often while you are in town. When you are comfortable, you can leave your brother's care to me. I assure you I will be only too happy to see him well situated before the Season's conclusion."

"Good heavens," John whispered. "Your condescension, Your Grace, is…that is, I cannot tell you how honored…your solution will do very nicely, Your Grace. I cannot thank you enough."

"Good. Will that suit you as well, child?" they said to me.

I nodded, feeling too shocked to speak. John elbowed me in the ribs.

"Thank you," I added hastily.

They chuckled. "It will be my pleasure. If you two are not otherwise engaged on Monday evening, you may join me for dinner. As I understand it, you are dining with Bertram tonight."

"Yes," I answered.

"The viscount?" John said.

The dukex nodded. "My cousin. He informed me that you were not free to join, Mr. Hartford. Ordinarily, I would have come in your stead, but I trust Bertram in this instance. As I understand, they have met several times by now. So if anyone asks, they can describe the meeting as one between friends."

"He informed you of it?" John said slowly.

"Yes. He asked if it would be proper to have your brother to dine alone since you could not join him."

John let out a long breath. "I am very relieved to hear that, Your Grace."

The dukex smiled. "I am glad to have met you, Mr. Hartford. Now I hope you both will excuse me. I have a social engagement and I must dress for it."

We all stood. John and I bowed. The dukex cupped my chin and said, "It was delightful to see you again, my dear." Then they left.

I followed John out of the house. "Now I really must meet that viscount tonight," he said when we got outside. "Is he as…"

"Terrifying?" I supplied. "No."

"Thank God," John said.

So last night I joined Viscount Finlington for dinner, alone. Charles wrote to him, apparently, and instructed him to look in on me. Finlington took that as a cue to invite me to dinner. He included John in his invitation, in case John took it into his head to come anyway. Fortunately, however, John only came long enough to meet him, before heading off to his own social commitment.

He was very civil to John, not giving away any indication that he had heard about him. Unlike Charles, he did not refrain from using terms of endearment around our brother. I think John was very shocked by it, but since Finlington addressed John as "m'dear" and "my sweet" as often as he did me, John forebore commenting. Thank goodness. He didn't even comment when Finlington proclaimed John to be as "charmingly attractive" as me. I'm sure John did not expect to be flirted with. It was rather funny, really.

I had told John the viscount ate early. This was Finlington's suggestion, by the way. He even said he thought it might make John approve of him. And it did! John told me he was pleased to know I had made at least two proper acquaintances while I was here and went so far as to say he wished he could know the viscount better. We didn't actually eat dinner until after seven, so it meant Finlington and I sat in his sitting room for some time simply talking. Once again, I am amazed at how much our brother's presence is driving me to do things I would normally shudder to do.

I was very awkward when I first sat down for I did not know how I would fill two hours of conversation, not to mention dinner and drinks afterwards. But Finlington had the matter well in hand. "How was your visit with my cousin?"

"Oh," I said. "It was very interesting."

He chuckled. "Charlie told me about all of your social callers and how much you were disliking the visits. I asked my cousin to call on you so that you might have a familiar face in the crowd."

"You did?"

He grinned at me. "They were only too happy to do it.

They've been quite annoyed that neither you nor Charlie have been present at any social functions lately. When I explained the situation, they were relieved you had a family member in residence. I also might have hinted that you were unhappy with your brother's company. So you can probably expect them to try to save you from that."

"Is that why they offered to be my chaperone?"

"Did they? Not entirely surprising. I would say it is one reason they offered."

"I don't understand all the fuss, quite frankly. I have not done anything untoward. Besides, my family sent me here on business. Isn't that generally an exception to the rule?"

"I know it, m'dear. And it is, generally speaking, an exception. But technically, Charlie probably oughtn't have taken you around town without another party, if only for the sake of your reputation." He held up a hand when I opened my mouth to disagree. "I know his behavior has been honorable, but not everyone knows this. And as a younger sibling, you will not reach your majority for another five years. So even if you do choose to act as your family's steward, which I believe is the business you are attending to, there ought to be someone around for propriety's sake. Even our dinner engagement really should include at least one other person. But I talked to my cousin about the matter beforehand and they agreed you deserved to have some space tonight. If you were to visit me again or more frequently, I would ask my cousin or your brother to join us. Otherwise, we might become the center of gossip." He paused and gave me a sympathetic smile. "You are so new to society, darling. I regret to say your reputation is rather fragile. Surely you can see the benefit of having the dukex looking out for your interests. They are a veritable leader in the fashionable world."

"Will they try to find me suitors?" I asked nervously.

"I don't think so," he said, looking as though he was

trying not to laugh. "You made your feelings on that offer quite clear."

"Oh, good," I said. "I am honored that they are willing to be my chaperone, but I hope you will not think me foolish for admitting I found your cousin to be very intimidating."

"Yes, they have that effect on people. They're an old softie underneath it all. And being in their company makes meeting new acquaintances significantly less frightening," he went on. "Everyone else is intimidated by the dukex too. So when they provide the introductions, most people will treat you with a great deal of respect."

I considered this. "I guess I can see that. Thank you, my lord."

"My pleasure," he said, smiling at me. "And I hope you won't mind, m'dear, if I pivot to a topic of particular interest to me. I should very much like to take the opportunity to discuss your magical abilities."

I blinked at him, completely taken aback by the topic. "Oh. Er. Why?"

He chuckled. "Well, from what Charlie has described, not to mention what we discussed at Vauxhall, I gather you have a very strong talent."

"Oh, I certainly wouldn't go that far, my lord," I said. "If anyone has a strong talent in the family, it's Gerry. That's my sister, you know. She's the one who has been learning about spell-building and whatnot."

"I am eager to meet her as well," he replied. "But you know there is potential for more than one strong spellcaster in a family, don't you? In fact, your sister's talents indicate a likelihood that power runs in your family. And besides," he went on before I could answer, "if I understand the matter correctly, she has been designing original spells and sending them to you. And then you have been casting them."

"Well, yes..." I said. "But they were no different than any other spell I've cast."

"The ability to pick up an entirely new spell and be able to cast it properly the first time is not exactly common, darling."

"Isn't it?"

He shook his head.

"I never thought it particularly extraordinary. I thought most people could do that."

"Most people can do common spells, particularly ones they've done before. To be able to pick up a complicated spell and do it without practice is a very good indication of talent."

"Oh," I said. "You sound very knowledgeable about such things, if you don't mind my saying so."

"Of course I don't mind you saying so, my sweet. I am something of an expert on magical abilities."

"You are?"

He nodded.

"I'm surprised I never heard about it."

He gave a small smile. "Well, to be perfectly honest, m'dear, it is not a widely known fact. I've worked rather hard to keep it that way. This isn't to say it's any sort of secret, necessarily. I have offered my expertise to Parliament and the crown whenever asked. But I think you will understand when I say I'm a fairly private person by nature. I do not mind society gossiping about me, but there are some things I do not wish to be used as fodder."

I was rather floored by this. "Does Charles know?"

He laughed. "You sweet thing. Yes, he knows."

"I write to my sister a great deal. Would it offend you if I mentioned it to her? She was very curious about you."

"Considering the fact that I fully intend to make her acquaintance, darling, it will not offend. But it is good of you to ask."

I nodded and tried to think of something to say.

"Charlie told me all about the heating spell she designed. Ingenious little invention, by the sounds of it. He says it kept the pot warm for an impressive amount of time."

"Yes, it was very well designed. It isn't even the first spell she's sent me and I was still amazed by it."

"What else has she sent you?"

"Well, there was really only the first one—a spell designed to extend the life of a candle. I was able to keep the same candle burning for seven or eight hours at a time for about a week. I asked her to send me another packet, but she never did. Although I suppose I have not had as much time for leisure since Charles—" I broke off, feeling myself blush.

"Since Charlie invaded your life and turned it completely upside down," he supplied. He chuckled at my expression. "It's what he does, darling. I hate to tell you, you might as well get accustomed to it. He's like that to everybody. Well," he went on. "Perhaps I ought to clarify. He is like that to everybody he cares for. If he sees a friend suffering from unhappiness, the dear man will do everything in his power to put the situation to rights. He is a good person to have liking you. But he can be a bit of a menace, you know, for he is incorrigible."

I huffed out a laugh. "Much as I hate to describe him as a menace, I must admit your description of him is apt."

"We've known each other since we were both in leading strings, m'dear. He's the very best person I know. But even I can tell you he is insufferable sometimes."

"Yes, I know. He made me take up boxing."

"He told me," Finlington said with a grin. "Between you and me, my sweet, I would guess that was due partly to ensure you were getting sufficient exercise and partly to see more of your adorable person."

I'm sure I was blushing bright red at this.

"Oh, forgive me, darling. I do say the most appalling things."

I shook my head. "I am too grateful to be out of John's company to be upset by it, my lord."

He laughed. "Call me Bertie, m'dear. I am sure we will be great friends."

"Thank you," I said (although, between you and me, Gerry, I'm sure I don't have the nerve to obey this request).

He gave me a warm smile. "How have you been surviving since Charlie left town?"

"My brother has been dragging me to all of his own social commitments. It has been dreadful. His friends are very dull. The only reprieve I've had all week was when I snuck away one night. Pretended to have the headache."

"You did mention that. Where on earth did you sneak off to?"

"Covent Garden."

He barked out a laugh. "Very clever spot, darling. I'm sure he never thought to look there."

"No, he didn't. And he's been keeping a close eye on me ever since, so it's been even worse. But I must say it was worth it. I cannot tell you how grateful I am to you for inviting me to dinner."

"You sweet thing, I was glad to do it. Truly. And I meant what I told you earlier: You are welcome to come here anytime. If I am not home, you can explore the library. I have a rather nice one and Charlie has mentioned you are a great reader."

I blushed again and looked at my lap. "Very kind of you."

"He's like a brother, you see," he said. "I know with certainty he would do the same for me. Besides, darling, you're such charming company, it is no hardship."

"You are very generous," I said. "I can't see how I have been anything like charming company to you. I barely talked most of the times we've met."

"Oh, don't worry about that," he said easily. "It was quite amusing really."

I huffed. "That's a surprisingly refreshing assessment.

John has been telling me this whole week how ill-mannered I am."

"I am sorry, darling. I wish I'd known to send for you sooner."

I shook my head. "It isn't your fault. I daresay I am a frightful coward for never telling John to—" I broke off and ran a hand through my hair. "Well, he is not my favorite topic of conversation. Would it be impolite of me to ask that we talk about something more pleasant? We can talk about Charles or you can tell me what you know of magic."

"Not at all, m'dear. I am glad you brought us back around to magic, actually. Would it make you uncomfortable if I asked you to perform a casting for me while you are here?"

I looked at him in surprise. "You want to watch me cast a spell?"

He nodded. "But only if you are comfortable with it."

"I suppose," I said. "But I'm really not as good as all that. I can't imagine it will be very interesting."

"Excellent!" he said. "Thank you very much, darling. Would you feel better doing it before or after dinner?"

I shrugged. "I don't have a particular preference."

"Why don't we go into the study then? I'll find a good spell for you to try."

I followed him out of the sitting room and down the hall to his study—a large room with tall bookshelves, a settee, a pair of wingback chairs, a globe, and a huge mahogany desk. There were all manner of tools and ingredients, and I was quite distracted by it all.

He pulled a book off the shelf and flipped through it. "How would this one do, dear?"

I took the book and looked over the spell. "I've never done it before, but it doesn't look too difficult." I frowned and looked at it more carefully. "Good heavens, must I draw a diagram for it?"

"Yes, darling. It is a combination of levitation and lateral movement. It is certainly an advanced piece, but there are no complicated calculations involved. All of the ingredients are fairly straightforward. We won't have to measure or weigh or treat any of them first, you see."

I nodded. "I can't promise I'll be able to do it, but I'm game to try."

"Marvelous." He glanced over the ingredients and began setting things onto the desk: chalk, a feather, a piece of reed, a ruler, and another book. "There now," he said, stepping back.

I picked up the book and began placing the ingredients as the spell indicated. Once I got to the diagram, I realized it was not so very complicated—it was merely an addition to the sigil to tell the magic in what direction the item needed to go. I measured the space from the spell to the desk and from the floor to the top of the desk. Then I chalked the measurements into the diagram. I was so nervous to have the viscount watching me that I went very slowly and carefully and double-checked everything. Then I cast the spell. As usual, I overpowered it, so the book landed on the desk with a large whack.

"Dreadfully sorry," I said, hurrying over to make sure I hadn't done any damage to the desk.

"Whatever for, darling?" he said, taking the book from me. "You did a marvelous job."

"I always put too much power into my spells, you see. It's a bad habit." I knelt on the floor and began to clean up the supplies.

He looked thoughtful as he knelt to help me. "Control can be learned. I'm sure you could master it fairly quickly if you put your mind to it and if you had the right sort of instruction."

"Really?" I said, sitting back on my heels. "My professors always gave me up for lost."

He rolled his eyes. "Most magical instructors know a very narrow sort of curriculum. Having so much power is decidedly not a bad thing. Moreover, you have very good instincts when it comes to spells. I did tell you it was an advanced one and you did it perfectly the first time." He held up his hand when I started to argue. "Truly, m'dear. It was perfectly executed. Yes, it was a trifle overloaded, but you could certainly learn to correct that."

"Oh," I said. "I confess I've never thought my spellcasting talents to be extraordinary."

"I imagine that is more from a modest personality," he said as he led me out of the study. "Your sister's spells might be well designed. But from your descriptions of them, I knew you had to have significant talent to have cast them so expertly. I've been hoping to talk to you about it ever since our conversation at Vauxhall. I'm grateful to you for indulging my curiosity."

"I'm just surprised it's anything impressive," I said. "I've always considered Gerry to be the talent in the family."

"From the sounds of it, she certainly is. But I expect she isn't the only Hartford who could make a career of such skills."

I stared at him. "You think I could?"

"Most assuredly, my sweet."

"I've been asking Charles for months if he had any suggestions for what career I might be able to take. How funny that you should have the answer all along."

He smiled as we returned to the sitting room. "Well, if you ask me, darling, I cannot imagine you will need a career in the end." Before I could reply to this observation, he continued, "But it is always good to know one's strengths. And, of course, one likes to have hobbies. If you ever desire additional training in terms of your control, I would be more than happy to assist."

"You would?"

"Gladly."

Dinner was called while I was still considering this offer.

He offered me his arm as he led me from the room. "I merely wanted to tell you it was an option, darling. I have a passion for training people in magic, you see. I like to see people recognize their own power and talent. But there is certainly no rush. I expect we will be seeing a lot of each other in the future." He smiled at me and said in a soft voice, "Charlie is very fond of you, you know. As I said before, I've known him for such a long time, he is practically family. So I hope you don't mind if I say I consider you practically family now too."

I took my seat, feeling a little awed. "I'm not sure I'm quite there yet."

"Oh, it's only a matter of time, my sweet," he said airily. "I know you are a private person as well, so I am sure you will wish to discuss a different topic now. How would you like to hear some anecdotes from Charlie's misspent youth, eh?"

I laughed and said I would love it. He didn't ask me any more personal questions the whole rest of the night and we talked about Charles for hours. It was wonderful, Gerry.

I stayed there until midnight and when I finally got home, John had fallen asleep on the sofa, trying to wait up for me. I was in such a good mood from my evening with the viscount that I was inclined to feel more charitably towards John than usual. So I gently shook him awake to tell him I was home.

He blinked up at me, bleary-eyed. "All right?" he murmured.

I nodded. "Just got home. I didn't want you to spend all night on the sofa. You'd never forgive me."

He shook his head in a vague sort of way and stood up. "Nonsense," he said. He rubbed his eyes. "Did you have a pleasant time?"

"Yes," I said. "He was very kind."

"Good," he said, yawning. "Let's go to bed. Is he always so flirtatious?" he asked as we walked slowly upstairs.

"I believe so," I said. "He's always been so with me. But I

don't think it means anything. I rather suspect it's just his way."

John nodded. "I suppose that's good. I was worried about leaving you unchaperoned, you know, regardless of what the dukex said. I almost cancelled my engagement, but it was far too late. And the hostess's daughter might be a suitable match for you. I didn't wish to insult her and ruin your chances."

"Oh," I said. "Er...thank you."

"If you were of the masculine persuasion, the viscount would be a very good match," he went on. "A bit eccentric, perhaps, but he could certainly support you financially. And if he is kind as you say, he would likely make a very good husband."

We were at the top of the stairs now. I did not know what to say to John in response. I was trying to determine if I ought to tell him my persuasion, but I was not really in the mood to have him lecture me on how I had been wasting his time.

"You know I only want you to be happy," he said in a quiet voice.

"Then why do you never ask me what would make me happy?" I said, matching his tone.

He rolled his eyes. "If you weren't so bloody tight-lipped all the time, I wouldn't have to guess. You make it infernally difficult to help you."

"I happen to think I don't need your help."

He huffed. "There you go, spouting foolishness again."

"It isn't foolishness," I said angrily. "I—" I broke off because I realized I had been about to tell him exactly why I didn't need his help, and all about my feelings for Charles, and my hopes to that end. But I had no desire to hear another diatribe on Charles's bad qualities. My good mood had completely evaporated.

He studied me for a long moment, frowning. Finally, he said, "It has not escaped my notice that a number of your callers are single gentlemen. Is there something you need to tell me, Gav?"

"No." I nearly ground out the word.

He sighed and pinched the bridge of his nose. "You are impossible. I'm far too tired right now. We'll discuss it later. Don't forget we're joining Hampstead tomorrow at that saloon of yours."

"I still don't see why you're bothering to go," I said. "You hate the very idea of boxing."

"Yes, well, you seem to enjoy it, so it won't hurt to see what all the fuss is about. Good night."

I shouldn't be surprised really that even when John has brief moments of seeming almost decent, he goes and spoils it. It is exasperating.

Let us both hope my next letter to you includes happier tidings.

Affectionately,
Gavin

FROM SEBASTIAN HARTFORD
Digory College, Oxford
TO GAVIN HARTFORD
8 Half Moon Street, London

29 January 1816

WHAT HO, GAVIN!

Do not, I beg of you, suggest to Father that I should leave school. Oxford is perfectly cracking! Why, just the other day, I cast the most hilarious little illusion spell. Made the entire fountain look as if it was full of bubbles. Best part was, there weren't any bubbles at all! So they would keep trying to clean it out. I nearly died from laughing! You see? No need to concern yourself!

What the devil is John doing in London? I declare, if he can dash about town when he has a newly born child, then I jolly well ought to be able to go too. Sometimes I think Father tells me no just to annoy me.

I don't know why you should be so coy on the matter of Mr. Kentworthy. Do you realize you referred to him by his first name in your previous letter? If you two aren't married, or at least engaged, the next time I see you, I'll eat my hat.

And you shouldn't be so very astonished. I have known your secret for years now. Some of us understand the art of subtlety, Gavin. Even if you do not.

Anyway, glad one of us is living the romantic life!

Now that you've gotten yourself squared away, would you be so kind as to keep an eye out for possible suitors for me? Better yet, would you be so kind as to tell *Charles* to keep an eye out for possible suitors for me? I may call him Charles, mayn't I? He's practically my brother, after all.

Pip now!

Seb

FROM GAVIN HARTFORD
8 Half Moon Street, London
TO GERALDINE HARTFORD
Shulfield Hall, Tutting-on-Cress

30 January 1816

DEAR, DEAR GERRY,

Bless you, my dear sister! Do you need any more fashion plates? I will send you a hundred of them if you like. Do they even make fashion plates at such a rate? I don't care. I'll find a way.

Under normal circumstances, I would wait upon your reply before writing to you again. But I'm tolerably certain you would never forgive me if I did not write to you immediately. Father wrote to John and—well, I had better start from the beginning.

I told you, I think, that I had started boxing more often at Muller's saloon after John insinuated himself into my London stay. For a little over a week, it kept me safely out of John's company. The other night, Hampstead came to dine and asked John why he never boxed. He told John it was "jolly good sport" and he was sure John would enjoy it. Well, after all his nonsense about Hampstead being an exemplary companion, John couldn't very well go on about boxing being vulgar. So he and Hampstead had decided we would all go together. As you can well imagine, I was not pleased. They'd both been accompanying me to my practice for days. For the most part, they kept in conversation with each other and John gave me some space to practice by myself. But today, Hampstead decided to include me in the conversation, much to my annoyance.

"How did you come to take up boxing then, little Hartford?" he asked.

"Mr. Kentworthy introduced me to it."

"Ah."

"You know Mr. Kentworthy?" I said.

"Only by reputation, of course," Hampstead said. "We do not go in the same circles."

"I should think not," John said. "My little brother has befriended the cad. I am trying to sever the association."

"Don't blame you," Hampstead said, looking at me in a strange way. "He's an odd fellow. Can't say I trust him."

"He's a dashed decent man. I would prefer it if you didn't speak of my friend in such a way."

"Of course," Hampstead said. "I would never *dream* of slighting another man's friend. But I think your brother is perfectly correct to discourage you."

"You see?" John said.

"Shall we begin our practice?" I said.

"You probably don't realize," Hampstead continued, ignoring my question, "but Kentworthy has something of a colorful reputation."

"So I've heard," I said. "It doesn't signify."

"But it does," Hampstead said, smirking. "If only half the stories were true, I should be ashamed to be seen with him."

"I imagine it would be the other way around," I muttered.

"Gav," John said in a warning tone.

"They say," Hampstead went on, "he hosts parties. Orgies, you know. Scandalous."

"Disgusting," John said.

"Fiction," I said.

Hampstead gave me a pitying look. "You're a little too young, I think, to understand. Too innocent. People like Kentworthy prey on boys like you, you know. Ingratiate themselves. It is very sad."

"How dare you suggest such a thing?" I said, feeling my face go hot.

"I'm surprised at you," John said. "It is not like you to take to anyone. Why are you so determined to think well of Kentworthy?"

"Why are you so determined to think ill of him?"

"Oh-ho!" Hampstead said, chortling. "I think I see which way the wind blows."

"What?" I said sharply.

Hampstead gave me another pitying look, the toad. "Don't you know? It's clear as daylight. You're in love with him."

I had, I'm ashamed to admit, nothing to say to that.

"Nonsense," John said.

Hampstead raised his eyebrows at me.

"It is hardly your affair," I said at last.

Hampstead laughed. "No, indeed. But, as a close friend of your family—indeed, we are practically family, you and I," he said as he proceeded to throw an arm over my shoulder in a brotherly fashion, "I feel bound to warn you to steer clear of Kentworthy all the same. He will eat you up, you know."

I shrugged him off. The room had gone silent and everyone was staring at us. I felt completely mortified, Gerry. Imagine having such a secret—I hadn't even managed to talk to Charles about it—joked about in public. I began to feel caged in and a little sick. I wanted to leave, but John put a restraining hand on my arm when I moved away from Hampstead.

"Is it true, Gav?" John asked me in a low voice.

"You know I hate to be called that."

His hand on my arm tightened. "Is this why you did not answer my letters? I told you Veronica offered to—"

"Oh, leave off, do," I said.

Hampstead sidled back up to us. "You see, Hartford?" he said. "This is why you could not persuade him better. The cub's smitten. I didn't know he was of that persuasion, m'self, but there's no doubt about it now."

"Why didn't you tell me?" John hissed.

"Poor thing," Hampstead continued. "You can't imagine he loves you back, can you? You're not the first boy he's seduced and I'm sure you won't be the last. He plows through affairs like a farmer, does old Kentworthy. I'm sure there's hardly a heart in London he hasn't bewitched."

"Do you hear, Gavin?" John said, still gripping my arm. "Kentworthy is not an honorable person. He will ruin you and your reputation, not to mention your future. A cad like him has no intention of being serious. I am sure you are just another toy to him."

"No decent person would have anything to do with him. If you have even a penny's worth of sense left in you, little Hartford, you'll listen to your brother and myself." Hampstead came to stand behind John, clapping him on the shoulder. "We know best."

"Yes," John said. "I'll help you find a more suitable gentleman."

"Anyone would be more suitable," Hampstead said. "Kentworthy's a bally whore."

"This is exactly why you should not have been left alone in London for so long," John said. "You are far too innocent for such things. It isn't the least bit surprising you fell prey to one of the most dangerous people in town."

I'm sure I should have kept my temper. I'm sure I should have ignored it. After all, it hardly matters what either of them think of anything. But I couldn't help myself; I was too angry. I was angry that John had so little respect for my judgment. Angry that he had dismissed Charles out of hand without even knowing him. Angry that he dared to lecture me on proper behavior when he was hiding in London from his wife and child because he could not bear to deal with his own responsibilities.

I punched him.

That is, I meant to punch John. But he saw me pulling my arm back and, for once, had the good sense to back away. So I punched Hampstead instead. This was not strictly my intention, but I had been wanting to punch Hampstead for some time anyway, so I did not exactly mind. He stumbled backwards and fell to the floor. John leaned over him solicitously before glowering at me.

"For God's sake, Gav," John said. "What has gotten into you?"

"Oh, stop it," I said. "Or I'll punch you too."

I felt a light hand on my shoulder and turned to see Charles standing at my side.

"You're back," I said. I own, it was a stupid thing to say.

"You did tell me to try finding you here when I returned to London. Everything all right?" he said in a low tone, taking in the scene before him.

"Oh, for goodness's sake. You're back," John said,

straightening up. I am pleased, Gerry, that I was not the only one to make inane observations at Charles's appearance. "Did you teach him this, Kentworthy? I daresay he never did any such things before his association with you."

I tensed and started forward, but Charles tightened his hand on my shoulder, keeping me back.

"And I daresay he never did it before you arrived in London, Mr. Hartford," Charles replied coolly. "Have I your permission to escort your brother back home?"

"I suppose," John said in a grudging tone. He managed to look down his nose at Charles again. "Mind you go straight home, Gav. No detours."

"Come," Charles said to me before I could reply. He swept his hand from my shoulder to the small of my back. "The fresh air will do you good."

He guided me to the dressing room, waved off the attendant, and then helped me to dress as if he were a valet. I dressed in a daze, too disoriented to take exception to his solicitousness. I wanted very much to ask him what he had heard and seen, and when he tied my cravat for me, I dearly wished to kiss him, which is most unlike me. But there were too many people about, so I simply stood quietly in front of him and then followed him out of the saloon.

As soon as we were out onto the street, he set a brisk pace. We did not talk for several blocks. I was still too stunned by his sudden arrival to say anything. Besides, there were too many things to say and I did not know how to articulate them. Nor did I particularly want to, not out on the street, I mean. I know Lino told me to be bold, but I hardly think he intended for me to make a public declaration.

Finally, when I couldn't take the silence any longer, I said, "How much of all that did you see?"

"None of it, really," he said. "I heard people shouting and when I got to you, Hampstead was stumbling backwards and you looked fit to murder someone."

"I felt fit to murder someone."

He glanced at me. "What happened?"

"They were insulting you," I said. "Both of them. John has been on this stupid bent that you're a bad influence on me and he's been trying to cure me of my friendship with you. I was actually intending to hit him. But I won't say Hampstead didn't deserve it."

Charles slowed and put his hand on my arm. "You were going to strike your brother because he was insulting my character?"

"Well," I said, shrugging. "It was more than that. Hampstead said horrible things about you, and John encouraged him. He doesn't have to like you, but the least he could—"

"You defended my honor?" Charles was grinning in that amused way of his.

"Well, someone had to."

"What exactly did he say?"

"Hampstead is dreadful, Charles. I have no desire to repeat the things he said about you."

"I hardly know the man," he said. "I'm a little surprised he should have such a strong opinion of me."

"It was awful. I couldn't get him to stop. And it only got worse when he realized that I—" I broke off suddenly and Charles gave me a sharp look. I felt myself flush and hurriedly looked away.

"Dearest," he said. I looked up and noticed his expression had softened. "It got worse when he realized what, Gavin?"

It was mortifying, Gerry. To have to tell someone such a thing. In the street. In public. In broad daylight. It does not bear thinking of. I had it all planned out in my head how I should say the words to him. Everything was going horribly wrong.

I looked at my feet. "Not here, Charles," I said.

He lifted my chin gently. "Please tell me," he said. "What did Hampstead realize?"

I swallowed. "That I love you, Charles."

Charles smiled that beautiful broad grin of his. "Darling," he whispered, and leaned in towards me.

I put my hand on his chest. "Not here," I said. "You don't actually mean to kiss me here."

"Whyever not?" he said, sliding his arm around my waist.

"People will talk."

"Don't they always?"

"We're not even engaged," I said.

He cocked his head. "Would you like to be?"

My arm went slack against his chest in surprise. "What?"

His grin widened. "I came back to London with no other intention than to ask for your hand. We can make it a long engagement, so you have time to get accustomed to the idea. Will you have me, my darling?"

"You cannot mean it," I said. "I am so very—"

He cast his face heavenward. "Do not, I beg of you, give me another soliloquy on your faults."

"But, Charles?"

He ran a hand through my hair. "Yes, my heart?"

"Why?"

"Because I love you, impossible man."

I had nothing to say to that.

When he saw I had no further arguments to offer, Charles took me into his arms and kissed me.

I should like to point out, Gerry, that even though you were not the first in our family to meet Charles, you are the first in our family to know of our official engagement. I hope this pleases you. It seems only fair, considering how much I have discussed him with you.

We stood on the pavement kissing for a shocking amount of time. Then Charles took my hand in his and started walking in the direction of the townhouse. It was lovely holding his hand. Add this to the list of things I never would have expected to have the courage to do before coming to London.

"How was dinner with Bertie?" he asked.

"It was very nice," I said. "He asked me to perform a spell for him."

Charles chuckled. "I should have warned you about that. He's an expert on the subject. I knew he would want to interrogate you about your abilities."

"I've never considered my abilities to be so very interesting before," I said. "So I can't say I minded it. He even said I could make a career out of it, if I wanted to." I paused. "But he also said he didn't think I would need one. Do you tell him everything?"

He gave me a rueful smile. "I do, darling. I am so sorry."

"I can't exactly complain," I said. "I tell Gerry a great deal too."

"Yes, I know."

"You have been writing to her!"

He laughed. "No, I really haven't. But I remember quite distinctly the way you dove for her letters with your last stitch of strength when you were ill."

I blushed and looked at my feet. "Oh," I said. "I'd forgotten about that."

"It was adorable," he said, squeezing my hand.

"Does Finlington know about my illness then?"

"Yes, and I very much regretted not telling him more about it. He would have likely diagnosed the problem sooner. I was a bit of a wreck, you know. So my letters were very brief. It wasn't until after your sister determined the source of the trouble that I wrote to him to verify her diagnosis. He was actually the one who made the antidote for you."

"You were a wreck?" I asked him quietly, catching on this particular detail.

"I was afraid I would lose you," he replied. He stopped and pulled me close for another kiss.

"Charles," I whispered. "Lino told me I would need to be bold and tell you everything I want to say, but...I can barely say the words 'I love you,' much less..." I floundered for a moment.

He gently kissed my cheek. "I know, my heart," he said. "There's plenty of time for you to say everything. I assure you I have much to tell you as well."

"You do?" I said, looking up at him.

"Oh, yes. I want to tell you how I couldn't take my eyes off you the first time I saw you. I want to tell you how sweet you look when you're focused on a spell. I want to tell you how much I love the way you blush. I want to spend hours and hours telling you everything I like about you." He pulled a little away and stroked my cheek with the back of his fingers. "I want to fill your head with so many good things about yourself that you turn a little prideful with it all."

"You're so much better at this than I am," I said. "I can't even—"

He touched a fingertip to my lips. "We have all the time in the world, dearest. I'm a patient man. You needn't say it all at once. Besides, you kiss quite eloquently."

I felt myself blush. "I do?"

"Oh, yes," he said, turning to lead me back down the sidewalk. "You kiss beautifully."

"That is nice to know," I said. "You were my first."

He smiled. "Another natural talent of yours then." He gave me a sidelong look and then said, "So, you went to Lino for advice, did you?"

"We just talked," I said hastily. "It wasn't—"

He laughed. "I'm teasing. Lino is very wise and a remarkably good judge of character. I'm pleased as anything that you recognized this in him."

"He had my measure the first time he met me, I think."

"Yes," he said. "He's like that."

I glanced up at him. "I imagine Finlington is too."

"Yes," he said with a grin. "He is."

"And the Dukex of Molbury as well?"

He sighed. "Yes. They are as well."

"They invited me to stay with them when John leaves."

Charles considered. "I confess I am not pleased by the notion of having to ask for permission every time I want to see you. But I also cannot deny that having their blessing in the matter would be very gratifying."

"Well, now that we are engaged, perhaps my staying with them will no longer be necessary."

He chuckled. "Actually, it will likely become more necessary. Now that my intentions have been officially declared, I cannot pretend we are spending time together simply as friends. I imagine Julian—that is, the dukex—will be relieved to learn about the betrothal, but they will want to see to it personally that your reputation stays untarnished."

"Oh," I said. "So I suppose I will have to stay with them then."

"It might be for the best. But I promise to visit you every day."

"You make it sound as if I'll be locked up in a tower or something."

He laughed. "It won't be that terrible. But if it helps, I'll gladly come on horseback to rescue you, my fair one."

I was about to object to his flowery language, but he lifted up our entwined hands and kissed the inside of my wrist. It felt intimate and thrilling and I nearly melted from the sensation. Naturally, I did not object to his wording after that.

By the time we made it back to the townhouse, John was already there and, unsurprisingly, in a foul mood. "What the devil took you so long?" he said.

"We walked," I said.

"It was an addlepated thing to do, you do realize. How am I to explain to Veronica that my brother struck her brother?"

"You might start by returning to her," I ventured.

He glared. "As it happens, I'm having my bags packed now."

"Oh," I said. "Are you?"

"Father wrote to me," he said. "Geraldine sent a letter to Mother and...well, Father told me to return right away. He threatened to come down and bring me back himself if I didn't. What a nuisance our sister is." His valet shuffled past us with John's bags and took them outside to the waiting carriage. "I have written to the Dukex of Molbury about my departure. See to it you thank them for taking you in. And make sure you behave properly."

I rolled my eyes. Charles gave my hand a squeeze.

John frowned down at our entwined hands. I was sure he was going to scold me about impropriety, but he said, "I do wish you would have told me it was more than friendship."

"Why?" I said. "Would you have been any less horrid if you had known?"

"I might...well, I might have tried a different tactic, surely."

"And now?" I pressed.

He let out a huff. "Well, it would seem that Geraldine went into a great deal of detail to our mother. Described my abuse of Mr. Kentworthy's character. Father read me a fine lecture. He said I was being unkind to the man who nursed you back to health last month." He ran a hand over his face. "For God's sake, Gav. If I had known all that, I would not have—"

"So you take it back, then? All those things you said?" I said.

"Well, as to that..." He gave Charles a hard look. "Gav is not the sort of person to let people in easily. I should know. I will not let him have his heart broken by a cad who doesn't care about him. Are your intentions toward my brother entirely honorable, sir?"

Charles grinned. "The most honorable, Mr. Hartford."

John let out a sigh. "Thank heavens for that at least. If you are in earnest, sir—"

"I am."

"Then, you ought to know, Kentworthy, my brother is the most stubborn person."

"He is indeed," Charles said, laughing.

John looked startled. He recovered his composure and said, "I expect I shall see you again soon then. I am sure you wish to meet our parents."

I scoffed. "Oh really, John."

"I would be delighted to come visit," Charles replied, ignoring me.

They bowed to each other then, with a little less stiffness than the first time they met. John patted my shoulder in what he probably thought was an affectionate way, and left.

Charles and I breathed a sigh of relief.

"Gerry saves the day," Charles said, smiling down at me.

"She tends to do that." I hesitated. "I should tell you. She knows. About us. I mean, I told her about, well, about before John arrived. About our kiss and everything."

"And?"

"Oh, she's terribly smug," I said. "Says she was certain it would happen. Described us like we were romantic figures in a novel. I shudder to think what she'll say when I tell her I punched Hampstead in your defense."

"What else did she say?" he said, running his free hand through my hair.

I narrowed my eyes at him.

"Well?" he said, dropping my hand and sliding his arm around my waist. He gently tugged me towards him.

This brought us closer together, which was pleasant, but also created the annoying predicament of having to tip my head back to see his face.

"Oh, very well," I said. "She said when we marry, she would like to come visit."

"That would be marvelous. And?" he said, kissing my cheek.

"And she wishes for me to bring you to our cousin's wedding in March."

"I would be delighted. What else?" he said, kissing my ear.

"She says my hair must have grown quite long for it to fall over my forehead so often but she says not to cut it as you appear to like it at this length."

He laughed into my hair and kissed my temple. "She's right, you know."

"She usually is," I said, tilting my head to look up at him.

"You really do tell her everything, don't you? Do you talk of me often in your letters?"

I laughed. "As a matter of fact, Charles, I talk of precious little else."

Then I kissed him.

Affectionately,

Gavin

EPILOGUE

From Charles Kentworthy, Esq.
  16 Berkeley Square, London
To Geraldine Hartford
  Shulfield Hall, Tutting-on-Cress

20 February 1816

My Dear Miss Hartford,

I was delighted to receive your letter of congratulations. Thank you kindly, my dear, for your sweet felicitations. I suppose you are right in saying it is not technically correct for us to start a correspondence without having formally met, but as we shall have the pleasure of meeting very soon, I do not see any harm in it. So please do not worry about any amount of judgment from my side. I have already enjoyed some correspondence with both of your parents since my engagement to your brother and I am eager for further acquaintanceship with everyone in Gavin's family. Besides, I have never been one for formality.

On that note, I would be delighted if you addressed me as Charles. I feel sure we shall get along famously and I do not see any need to bog down the proceedings with proper address. From what Gavin has told me of your character, I feel reasonably confident you will not be opposed to this suggestion.

You can expect your brother and I to arrive on the first of the month. We intend to stay a fortnight in Tutting-on-Cress at your aunt's house, in order to attend the wedding and meet everybody. After that, we plan to visit your parents. As I understand it, you have been away from home since the summer, so if you wish to travel with us, I would be delighted to include you in our party. I should add that Gavin has mentioned your eldest brother will be taking his own family to stay with his in-laws for a few months. Both his wife and son will be well enough to travel by then, and I take it her parents are eager to see their grandson. I do not wish to presume, of course, but I would hazard a guess this might sway your own decision. We shall stay a fortnight with your parents and then travel on to Bath for a week or two. I am eager to introduce Gavin to my aunt. After that, I intend to return us both to London for the Season.

Speaking of which, my dear, if you plan to return to London for the Season as well, I would be delighted to act as escort. Your mother has hinted in her own letters to me that she would appreciate my assistance in this matter. However, I do not wish to encourage the notion without your blessing. I am confident I could acquire a good number of invitations to a variety of social functions for your benefit. I do not know what your brother has told you of our time in London, but rest assured any descriptions of bullying him or dragging him about town have been grossly exaggerated. I can safely promise to be a charming companion and to see to it you are introduced to as many delightful bachelors as you might like. I should also note that Gavin will most certainly be accompanying us on these adventures, lest you fret about being taken about by a stranger. I imagine he will put up some amount of fuss at this prospect, but I simply cannot resist the temptation to introduce the dear man as my betrothed to as many people as possible.

You are likely already aware of your brother's move to the Dukex of Molbury's residence. I ought to warn you that the dukex will undoubtedly extend the same invitation to you if you return to town. They have all but adopted Gavin at this point, and it is evident they are thoroughly enjoying playing the role of chaperone. So you can probably expect similar treatment. Quite frankly, you can also expect the dukex to accompany us on most of our excursions in London. I have already had to resign myself to that reality.

My other reason for writing to you is to request some advice. As I will be meeting a great many of Gavin's relatives in the next month, I would dearly like to make a good impression and have a mind to bring some gifts along for the journey. Gavin tells me this is thoroughly unnecessary, but it has been years since I've had a family to call my own and I'm determined to start off on the right foot.

Since I cannot depend on your brother for an opinion, would you be so kind as to recommend what your aunt, uncle, cousins, parents, and brothers might like? And, of course, darling, you are most assuredly on my list of recipients. I have already acquired some lovely fashion plates for you, but if there is anything else you would like, please do not hesitate to tell me. Perhaps some ingredients for your magical experiments? I do not know what your spellmaster has in stock in Tutting-on-Cress, but anything that can be gotten in a London spell shop is yours for the taking, my dear. Simply tell me what you would like. If you do not have anything particular in mind, I will ask my friend Bertie what might be most useful to you.

I look forward to your reply and look with even more anticipation still to our meeting. As I'm sure you know, dearest Gavin is not forthcoming on most subjects, but he has always been particularly keen to discuss you. I feel as if we are friends already, my dear. Between you and me, thank you from the bottom of my heart for every encouragement and advice you have sent to Gavin in the past few months. He depends upon you a great deal, you know. I would be a fool to believe our engagement was solely due to my own charms and efforts. I am certain you played a large role in my current happiness. So, thank you, dear, dear Gerry, for every letter you sent to your brother at Half Moon Street.

With love,

Your future brother-in-law (my word, darling, but it feels so good to write that!),

Charles Kentworthy

~

The End

NOTE FROM THE AUTHOR

DEAR READER,

This book was borne out of my reading Georgette Heyer Regency romances and several queer romance novels simultaneously. As a queer writer with a love of historical romances, I wanted to create Regency romance novels that were sweet and fluffy. Once the fantasy element made its way in, as it normally does in my writing, I realized I could make my universe as queer-friendly as possible. Everyone deserves to see characters they relate to and I believe there is great value in seeing such characters in safe and loving settings. I hope you enjoyed reading Gavin and Charles's story as much as I enjoyed writing it.

Thank you for joining me on this journey. I am looking forward to telling you more stories in the future.

Affectionately,
Sarah Wallace

ACKNOWLEDGMENTS

This book wouldn't exist without my amazing friends who have supported me every step of the way. For my beta readers, Ashley, Alexis, Kayla, Emily, and Lauren, I cannot tell you how much your feedback helped to improve this story. Thank you to my editor, Mackenzie Walton, who provided me with a much needed objective and professional viewpoint. Thank you to Cath Liao at Salt & Sage Books for answering all of my questions. Thank you to Ashley for helping me get my book to a more polished state. Thank you to Alexis for acting as a sounding board when I incorporated a new element to the world building. Thank you to Emily for telling me what I needed to hear to self publish this book.

Editor: Mackenzie Walton
Proofreader: Ashley Scout
Historical Consultant: Alexis Howard
Sensitivity Reader: Cath Liao at Salt & Sage Books
Front cover photo by Stephen Packwood via Unsplash
Back cover photo by Black Chitsulo via Unsplash
Author photos by Toni Tillman

ABOUT THE AUTHOR

 Sarah Wallace lives in Florida with her cat, more books than she has time to read, a large collection of classic movies, and a windowsill full of plants that are surviving against all odds. She only reads books that end happily.

Printed in the USA
CPSIA information can be obtained
at www.ICGtesting.com
LVHW091145170923
758440LV00024B/400

9 781737 432708